THE AGORA LETTERS

5 Historical Murder Mysteries

CLAY BOUTWELL

www.ClayBoutwell.com

———

Visit the author's website at http://www.ClayBoutwell.com

ISBN-13: 978-1548111878
ISBN-10: 1548111872

DOWNLOAD AN EBOOK FOR FREE

How about a free eBook copy of Clay's Superhero thriller
Carritos The Assassin?

Get the PDF, Kindle, and ePub versions for FREE. Join the
exclusive First Readers Club, get coupons, and learn about
exciting new titles before everyone else.

VISIT
WWW.CLAYBOUTWELL.COM
TO GET YOUR **FREE** COPY TODAY.

VOLUME 1: TWO TOCKS BEFORE MIDNIGHT

The Agora Mystery Series

❧ I ❧

October 24th, 1889
Carl Brooke
Boston

I HAVE NEVER BEEN FOND OF SENTIMENTAL RAMBLINGS SO I will keep this short. Indeed, were it not for the insistence of my friends, I would soon let the matter slip away with the sands of time. But repeated pleas from the curious and the morbid alike compel me to share with you the strange affair of October 24th, 1859.

I cannot say with certitude the events of this date occurred exactly as I remember them. As time passes, so do the minute and myriad details; rough edges are made smooth, and the inevitable romanticizing of the past is liable to play havoc with true fact.

Still, as I am a Christian and an honest man, what follows is as accurate as my fallible mind can relate.

Nearly two score years separate us from those days and

that night in particular. I, alone—so I am told—am survived out of the lot of us.

Before I begin to describe the events of that night, I think it important to share a little more about our group.

We were the *Agora Society*, an open marketplace to foster ideas for the betterment of man. That was the aim; the structure, however, was modeled after Dr. Franklin's *Junto Society*. In a show of hubris that even today causes me to shudder with embarrassment, our charter set forth the goal of leaving to the world a greater legacy than that of the good Doctor. Indeed, we had the mind to compete with the man who "took lightning from the sky and the scepter from the tyrant's hand" as Turgot put it. He surely laughs at my friends in the hereafter. I fear there are times when I hear his laughter echoing in my dreams, beckoning for me to come.

I do not think it wrong, however, to recollect our accomplishments—as dim as they may be when held up to Dr. Franklin's light.

During the years of our club's existence, we established a Freeman's society which secured the release of one hundred and thirty-six slaves. We also ensured these men and women were taught a trade and their letters. It is of considerable pride to report nearly all of them transitioned well after the War between the States. Indeed, several families prospered. To this day, I have no greater joy than to receive a letter or a visit from a member of one of these families.

Another source of pride came when the Society financed the repairing of the dam in Clarkesville, which was completed a mere month before the great flood of fifty-six. Over the years, we were involved with building libraries, windmills, schoolhouses, and churches.

It is also true that our services were used on a number of occasions by the police, as this letter will attest. Though small, we were well-connected and able, by merit of our collective talents, to be of some value to law enforcement.

In short, our efforts saved the lives of hundreds of mortal and immortal souls. However, again remembering our foolish goal, Dr. Franklin's invention of the simple lightning rod alone, has surely saved millions.

Our society, the *Agora Society*, had a dozen members at its zenith. Each brought to the group his individual talents and ambitions. Mine lay in ancient Near Eastern languages.

To give a brief sampling of the others pertinent to our discussion, my dear friend, Dr. Christopher Harding, an expert in papyrus, cuneiform, hieroglyphics, and other writing methods of antiquity, led the initial discussion of the matter; Mr. Thomas Phillips, knowledgeable in ancient warfare and weaponry, could always be heard quoting some obscure Greek or Roman philosopher; and of course, Mr. Charles Tock could converse in thirteen languages and read five more. Charles Tock and Thomas Phillips are of special interest to our story.

The weekly meetings were held every Monday evening at precisely six of the clock. If someone was absent or tardy, he was made to do "community service." This usually meant clearing the streets of horse manure. The delights of such an occupation was a great incentive to arrive on time, and it was a rare occasion when one of us failed to do so.

Charles Tock joined our august group a few years before the events of that dreadful night. I should note, as a matter of protocol, we referred to each other by our first names no matter our age or status outside the *Agora*. I distinctly remember Charles' introduction the first evening he appeared before our group. I relate it now because it accurately illustrates his dry humor and the breadth of his academic knowledge.

"My name is Charles," he said, pausing to allow his eyes to

greet each of us. "That can't be helped, but I always intended to marry royalty to avoid being churlish."

Only a few of us caught the etymological jesting. Having a name, Carl, that shares the same cognate as Charles, namely "churl," I was one of them. "Churl," as you know, came to mean the opposite of nobility, a rude man somewhat above a peasant.

Despite his poor taste in arcane humor, Charles' broad knowledge and experience soon propelled him to something of an elder position among us—a natural state of affairs, since the majority of us were more than two decades his junior.

In the years since these events, many people have asked me if we suspected anything unusual about him from the beginning. In retrospect, he could be willing to compromise his principles to achieve his aims. He had demonstrated this vice in small ways over the few years we knew him, but so subtle and inconsequential were these incidents, no one made mention of them in complaint. None of us could have anticipated his spectacular downfall.

He arrived suddenly, and one winter morning, left just as suddenly—and without telling anyone. As I have already attested, missing even a single meeting was heavily discouraged. This transgression was doubly shocking considering how integral he had made himself to the club.

On the third meeting after his extended absence, we decided a party should be sent to learn what had become of him. The talk of discipline from the week before turned to genuine concern. I was not among those chosen to join the search party, but I did receive their report. Charles' lodgings —the address he gave in the society's records—was an abandoned slaughterhouse. As it turned out, no member had visited Charles outside club meetings during the entire time he had been with us. Being a band of honorable men, we took our members word as fact. This trust, unfortunately, allowed opportunity for abusers.

But the mystery had only begun.

Winter turned to spring, and spring to summer. It is difficult to overstate our total and utter amazement when a full six months after his disappearance, Charles Tock quietly walked through the doors of the *Agora Society* once more. Bearded and dirty, he wore a tattered frock coat and carried a lantern that cast a circle of yellow light, illuminating his features. He looked churlish to say the least.

While not against club rules, facial hair was a rarity among us. Only one of us, Thomas Phillips, had a neatly trimmed mustache. The rest of us, during those days, were clean-shaven and therefore seeing Charles with an abundance of facial hair was doubly shocking.

With him stood a large, similarly dressed man in dark clothing carrying a leather case with a large brass buckle.

A hushed pause descended as we all turned and stared at the strange sight.

☙ 2 ❧

Please allow me to indulge in a little narrative. While the phrasing may be somewhat inaccurate, I shall be as true to my memory as my venerable age allows.

"CHARLES, WHERE THE DEVIL HAVE YOU BEEN?" ONE OF US blurted out.

He walked to the front and set his lantern on the table. His companion remained near the entrance.

"I've been traveling. This is... Joseph," Charles answered while nodding toward the large man to his side. Charles looked as though he had aged ten years. Beads of sweat rolled down his cheeks and into his beard. This was not odd considering the heat of the summer, yet, somehow, the sweat seemed to be of a different sort.

We were in shock, both by Charles' unexpected return after these many months of absence and by the presence of this stranger, a clear violation of the society's charter.

"Charles, there are certain rules with which you must

surely be acquainted," I said, trying to admonish him as lightly as I could.

"Joseph will leave shortly, but he has something that will undoubtedly be of considerable interest to all, and, Carl, to you in particular."

Our interest piqued, the president motioned for Charles to step forward and address the meeting. Charles nodded and moved to the front while patting his forehead with a handkerchief.

"I do apologize for the abrasive nature of my reappearance. It was unavoidable, I'm afraid." He paused to once again pat a fresh bubbling of sweat. It seemed some heaviness hindered him from continuing. Surely hidden from the crowd, but not from me, Joseph move his fist slightly, prompting Charles to continue. "Yes, well, Joseph, please present the document."

The room was quiet save for the striking of a clock and the occasional hawker announcing his wares on the street below. I doubt any of us noticed those things, however. Such was the tense atmosphere.

With rough movements, the stranger pulled a parchment from his case. Even from that distance, the manner in which he handled what seemed to be an ancient document brought a shudder to my frame.

Contrary to club protocol, I pushed through the others to observe the object closer. Dr. Christopher Harding, the expert on papyrus and other ancient writing utensils, was equally inquisitive and also stepped forward.

The scroll was clearly ancient, and the writing, Paleo-Hebrew. The sheepskin had been prepared in the proper way as befitting an ancient Torah scroll. But it most certainly was not a Torah scroll.

"Can you read it, friend?" Joseph grunted, baring his

teeth. The tone, rather than the words, betrayed an aggressive impatience.

My hand trembled as fingers hovered an inch above the precious parchment. Christopher examined the physical document, devoting special interest to the edges and damage wrought by countless years. I, meanwhile, studied the language.

"My word," Christopher said. "Where did you discover this?"

"A dig in the Middle East," Joseph answered before Charles could open his mouth. Neither man elaborated further.

"What is it?" a member asked.

It seemed the entire room refused to breathe until we made known the contents of the parchment.

"It is a... *gevil*," Christopher answered, "written in the Paleo-Hebrew script, but as to the contents, you will have to ask Carl."

Christopher's matter-of-fact response of a *"gevil"* remained unsatisfactory for our fellow members unschooled in ancient writing materials.

I explained. "A *gevil* is a specially prepared animal skin used by Jewish scribes, particularly for Torah scrolls."

"Is it, then, a Torah scroll?" asked one member.

"No."

I wasn't sure what it was, but it was no Torah scroll. Christopher handed me a magnifying glass and backed away, giving me room for the examination. I said nothing for a few minutes and, understanding my need for concentration, no one spoke or made a sound.

"A Bible, please," I asked.

We kept a large Bible on the shelf inside the stand for the initiation ceremony and for occasional reference. It was handed to me and I consulted two places to confirm my memory.

"Most extraordinary." The elation I felt at that moment brought forth a grin to my face I could not contain.

"My dear, Carl," said Christopher, eyes wide and glowing with anticipation. "Please do not keep us in suspense. I shall have to leap from London Bridge if you are not forthright this moment."

"My apologies, Christopher. Based on your experience, how old would you say the parchment may be?"

Christopher cleared his throat before answering. "It would be impossible to know for sure. The quality is unsurpassed. Lesser specimens would still have traces of animal hair. Clearly, this was from a roll and not a codex which would be similar to a modern book. In general that suggests pre-fifth century A.D., but I dare not hazard a more specific guess."

"Would you say... mid-ninth century is possible?" I asked, perhaps a little too playfully.

"Yes, but as I mentioned, as it is from a roll, pre-fifth century is..."

"No, my good man," I said, raising my eyebrow and managing to wipe the smile from my face. "Not A.D. The ninth century B.C."

A hush fell around us as all waited for Christopher to respond. Only the hiss of the two gas lamps on the wall broke the silence.

"Yes," he said, bracing his arms on the table for support. "It is possible. The parchment is in very good shape, but if it had been kept in a dry, cool storage and undisturbed... yes, it is possible. But how can you be so specific?"

"The corner," I said, pointing to the lower left area. "Can you read it?"

The line wouldn't have given pause for someone with even rudimentary Hebrew.

"*Melech*," he said after sounding out the three characters. "*Achazyah... Chai. Melech Achazyah Chai!*" His arms flew up and his eyes danced with excitement. "My dear fellows," he said turning to the other men who had—against all society etiquette—crowded around us with the greatest of curiosity. "King Ahaziah lives! This was written during the reign of the great, great, great, great, great grandson of King David. Mid-ninth century B.C. would be on target."

"The Paleo-Hebrew style is consistent," I said finding it increasingly difficult to withhold my excitement.

"But," spoke up one of the men behind me. "What of its contents?"

I answered promptly. "There is little doubt. I have only had a few minutes to examine it, but if I had to make a judgment this very moment, I would have to say this may well be a segment of the *Sefer HaYashar—the Book of Jasher.*"

I went to explain the Book of Jasher was one of the "lost" books from the biblical period, being named in scripture but no longer extant. When the sun stood still for Joshua, the book is mentioned for further reference. David bade them to teach the sons of Judah the use of the bow as mentioned in this book.

"If memory serves, Josephus said the Hebrews stored the Book of Jasher in the temple nearly two thousand years ago. It was thought lost after the destruction of Jerusalem in seventy A.D.," added someone.

Charles seemed relieved, but somehow unhappy. Joseph smiled as he spoke, "Would you, then, gentlemen, certify its authenticity?" Just as before with "friend," the way he muttered "gentlemen" seemed somehow quite unfriendly.

Thomas Phillips, who had been one of the more excitable among us regarding the parchment, spoke: "It would be our honor, wouldn't it, boys?" His curled mustache wiggled with the words.

I held up a cautious hand. "My good fellow, I would love to—upon further examination, of course. I must study the text in detail and compare it with other so-called '*Books of Jasher*' discovered in the last century.

Joseph's smile dropped and he snatched his lantern from the table. "You have an hour. I shall return to collect the parchment then." With that, Joseph and Charles were gone.

I spent the next few minutes rapt in joy. The others took turns peering over my shoulder or standing in front, occasionally interrupting my examination with their comments—sometimes helpful, sometimes not. It had grown too dark for the wall lamps by that time and two candles were brought near to illuminate the text.

Only after half an hour of study did I discover something that would condemn three souls to their deaths.

❧ 3 ☙

I felt the blood drain from my face as I gripped the edge of the table in a vain attempt to steady my nerves.

"What is the matter, Carl?" asked Christopher.

One heavy heartbeat later, I responded. "I... I am afraid there may be a problem."

I pointed to two Hebrew letters and asked Christopher to read them.

"Yes, yes," Christopher replied. "It is the common Hebrew word '*shel.*' It means 'of' or 'belonging to.' What is your point?"

"'*Shel*' is a syntactical innovation of a much later date."

Never have I felt such deep disappointment befall so many people as a result of my words.

"Not only that, Christopher," I said, handing him the magnifying glass. "Look closely at the ink here and here."

Christopher took the glass and bent over the parchment.

"My word. I didn't see it before, but while the parchment does appear to be quite old, the writing seems to be newer. The flaking here," he said, pointing to a tiny area missing some ink, "indicates the ink has not had time to bond. And here, we see a scratch in the parchment running through this aleph and yet the ink is unharmed. Good eye, Carl."

"And," I said, driving the last ounce of doubt from my mind, "if held against the light, one can see nearly invisible pencil marks—very modern pencil marks, undoubtedly a practice run before inking."

We were all, of course, greatly disappointed, but in the end, we agreed the specimen was nothing but a clever fraud. Even Thomas Phillips who had offered the best counter-arguments eventually conceded after facing the overwhelming evidence.

Our name would not be soiled, but we would have to break the news to Charles and Joseph. By their reactions, we expected to determine whether they had foreknowledge of the forgery.

A FEW MINUTES LATER, JOSEPH RETURNED WITHOUT Charles.

"Well?"

"I'm afraid," I said, speaking up as the representative of our club, "you have a clever forgery here."

"What do you mean?" Joseph's mouth shut tight and his eyes turned blood-red.

"I mean, the text cannot be but a few months old," I said, returning the carefully rolled parchment to him.

Joseph clenched his fists and then relaxed them, apparently thinking better of it. He snatched the parchment and stormed out without a word or a tip of his hat.

❧ 4 ❧

The excitement produced by Charles and Joseph filled the club with talk the next week, but it was soon forgotten as time passed. We were concerned about Charles of course, but as before, we had no idea where to find him. No one wanted to say it out loud, but we all suspected Charles of having a hand in creating the forgery.

Weeks passed and then months. One day, a member arrived at my door rather agitated. He told me he had been traveling to Chelsea and discovered the very parchment Joseph and Charles had brought. It was on display at a museum—which museum, I will not say out of respect for the director.

We immediately called the others, and the majority instantly decided to make the journey to the museum. Thomas, despite being one of the more excited among us when we believed the parchment to be authentic, declined to go.

On close examination, it was not the same parchment as the forgery presented to us by Charles and Joseph, but it had similar content. We were amazed to find out many—but not all—of the flaws we discovered were absent. This parchment was clearly a second attempt and a much better one.

The museum director was far from pleased. With his gracious permission, we collected all the information we could about this strange forgery and its creators.

In addition to Charles Tock and Joseph, the director mentioned another man had been among those who had sold the parchment to the museum. The group went by different names, but a quick description of their physical attributes and mannerisms left little doubt as to the identity of two of the forgers. The third man—unknown to us—added to the mystery.

About the same time, one of our number discovered an advertisement in the prestigious *Journal of Antiquity*. A New York book dealer was offering a parchment from the *Book of Jasher* to "some museum or lover of the classical Biblical world" for four hundred dollars.

Taking an extended absence from our responsibilities, Christopher and I made the two hundred mile journey by rail and stagecoach and met the man. He had, of course, bought the parchment from Charles, Joseph, and the third man, the forgers once again presenting false names. Once more, we discovered a clever forgery that showed a marked improvement in skill on the part of the forgers. I dare say, an expert not having been privy of the previous attempts would have been fooled.

Charles Tock had considerable talent, but we wondered whether he alone could have created the forgeries. They were, after all, marvelous in design and, while skilled in modern languages, Charles was not known to be a biblical language scholar. Joseph did not leave the impression of being a scholar at all, and we therefore surmised this third man, whoever he may be, must have possessed the requisite talent in this regard.

I then realized the whole matter if left unchecked would blur the lines between truth and falsehood. Through books and articles, these forgeries had the power to influence scholarship for years to come. The criminals had to be stopped and we, experts in our fields, were best suited to complete the task.

Back at our weekly club meeting, I suggested our society should direct all its collective energies and talents into bringing the rogues to justice. We all were in agreement, except Thomas—who, at the time I assumed, was ashamed of his impetuous rush to authenticate the parchment and simply wanted to put the matter behind him. However, we could not tolerate deliberate falsehoods. With Charles Tock having been one of our members, we all felt a tinge of responsibility.

Immediately, our club journeyed to every museum and antiquities dealer or collector within a hundred-mile radius. We sent letters warning museums far and wide about the *Book of Jasher* forgeries. We took out advertisements in every journal and newspaper in the region. In all, our group invested hundreds of hours and dollars into the project.

After a few weeks, we ceased our efforts, convinced we had done our part to warn the public.

Unfortunately, this was only the beginning of the affair.

Once again, Charles reappeared just as suddenly as he had disappeared, but not in a way any of us would have wished.

It was the night of October 24th, 1859.

As it happened, I was on key duty that month, which meant I was to arrive early to open the meeting room and leave late to lock up.

As was required of me, I showed up early to unlock the room and prepare for the meeting. Thomas Phillips—who was known to be punctual but never early—was at the door, waiting for me.

"Carl, how are you this evening?"

"Fine. Fine. Shall we enter?"

I proceeded to open the premises and walk inside. Hearing a creaking, I looked up and in the stale light seeping through the curtained windows, I saw Charles hanging from the rafters, dead. His corpse swung slightly, and on his chest, I noticed someone had attached a note.

Thomas rushed to the body, steadied the swinging, and snatched the note.

"Carl, it simply reads, 'Two Tocks Before Midnight.'"

With no overturned footstool beneath the body, we quickly determined, to our horror, a crime had been committed. This was no suicide. Someone had murdered Charles Tock.

The police did not take long to reach the premises. Fellow members poured in, each wearing concerned and stern faces, as we explained the situation to them. Immediately, we all suspected the mug who had accompanied Charles the night of the parchment: Joseph.

To the best of our abilities, we each described him to the police detective, Captain Barnwell.

If you will forgive the momentary digression of an old man, Captain Barnwell became a close friend of the Society and it behooves me to take some time to describe the fellow.

Tall and ruddy in the face, he showed great aptitude in both his mental and physical faculties. His appearance seemed more of an athlete than a police captain, but this man with the body of a sprinter housed the mind of a quick-witted scholar.

During the length of our acquaintance, Captain Barnwell wore a large mustache which effectively masked his emotional state as well as his upper lip. One could never be certain the cards the captain held until he laid them on the table and the ends of his mustache wiggled accordingly.

You may never find a man with greater contrasting qualities. He was reticent to a fault regarding the social graces, but when the topic of crime arose, he shared his opinions with shocking celerity. Of popular literature and theater, he knew nothing and cared even less, but of the latest scientific discoveries—especially such as showing promise for use in deterring criminal activity—he was well versed.

I made mention of his mustache and to his mustache, I must return for it was his greatest detecting tool. During the questioning of a suspect, no matter how tight-lipped the man may have been, any falsehood or irrelevant fact was greeted with a twitching of his facial hair and with it, a most deprecating frown, from which few questioners could maintain deceit. In numerous examples through the two decades of our friendship, I saw that man with his mustache wiggle out the truth in the most amazing ways.

Captain Barnwell leveled his mustache and applied his business-like eyes to some notes in his hand; his words, however, were directed to me. "You say this Joseph fellow seemed belligerent and treated Mr. Tock roughly?"

"Yes, that is correct," I answered. "In addition, two of the purchasers of a parchment mentioned a third man. We have no idea who he is, but he could have been the mastermind behind the forgeries and perhaps this." I pointed to the body which lay upon a canvas sheet on the floor.

"Two Tocks Before Midnight," said the captain. "What the devil could that mean? Charles' last name, of course, was Tock. Could it mean one of his relatives?"

After a quick consultation with the others, I spoke up. "We have never met any of his relations. He kept to himself and never spoke of anyone to go home to."

"Before midnight," said Christopher. "Wouldn't that imply that something will occur *tonight* by midnight? Could 'Two

Tocks' mean, 'two deaths like Tock' and these deaths would occur shortly before midnight tonight?"

It seemed a sensible interpretation. If so, we had less than six hours to prepare.

The group grew silent. And then, after some discussion, we decided, in the interest of safety, that all members would spend the night in the society room. Those with family were encouraged to bring their loved ones or take them to a place of shelter. Whoever the murderer happened to be, he was able to freely enter the club room where we stored the records and addresses of members.

I then remembered that over the years Charles had been with us, he had only recommended one fellow to join our ranks. We'd had no objections and he was quickly ushered in. That fellow was Thomas Phillips, the very same man who had entered the room with me and had co-discovered the body.

I searched for Thomas but could not find him. I further remembered he had been the only member to be overly eager to certify the authenticity of the parchment before it could be properly examined.

"Christopher," I waved until I raised his attention, "a word, please."

We huddled in a corner as I expressed my concerns. We both commented on how quiet he had been and we speculated that he might actually be a relative of Charles. If so, his life could be in danger.

We called the others and caught the captain before he left. As with Charles, it turned out the society records had a false address for Thomas: 114 Elm Street. One of our members lived nearby and assured us Elm Street only reached number 110.

Someone remembered seeing him at a bank as a teller. By this time, the clock had struck six, but we managed to track down the bank's manager who, after much pleading, opened the bank and gave us the address on file for Thomas. The address given was the same: 114 Elm Street.

Thomas had been introduced by Charles, and like Charles, he had given us a false address. He arrived early to be the first to discover Charles' body and then had promptly disappeared. All evidence seemed to indicate he was part of the plot. But was he the murderer or now a target—the second *Tock*?

Concerned, I considered the encounter with the body of Charles. It had been swinging slightly. Perhaps, the murder had just occurred. With further consideration, all doubt fled my mind. Charles must have died mere minutes prior to our entering the room. When cutting Charles down, the corpse had been warm. Thomas had been there before me and in my memory he had been in a state of agitation. He could have retained a key to the room. He could have entered with Charles and murdered him there. It seemed the most likely explanation as I had seen no one else in the area.

By eleven o'clock, we had regrouped and all members waited in the club meeting room. Thomas was still absent as were a few other members—mostly those with families.

Due to the extraordinary situation, the fact the killer potentially had studied our personal addresses, and the specific time given for the promised crime, Captain Barnwell dispatched officers to each of our houses to watch the homes. We warned the police that Thomas was an expert with weaponry and may be armed.

Christopher pulled me aside. "Do you not remember the key passage from the parchment? '...only teach thy sons the use of the bow and all weapons of war.'"

"Yes. The bow. Thomas once spoke of his collection and how he enjoyed hunting with nothing more than a bow and a quiver full of arrows."

Christopher talked to the others about our little theory

while I searched the room. We had but two links to the outside: the door and a single window. We were on the second floor over an antique bookseller's shop. The window would only be a danger if a shooter were to be located in the apartments across the street.

The door was constantly opening and shutting even at that late hour—far too many people were coming and going bringing in family members or looking outside. The police were also entering and leaving, asking for more information about Thomas. I realized we needed the door locked with everyone inside immediately.

Then, a thought caused my frame to shiver: the killer had entered through the locked door once before.

"Barricade the door and stand clear of the window!" I shouted to everyone's alarm.

Before my instructions could lead to action, at precisely half an hour before midnight, Thomas reappeared.

Conversation ceased, and all heads turned to face him.

"I do apologize for my late arrival." Clearly seeing he had everyone's total attention, he continued, "I wanted to arrive earlier, but I had to make sure my property was secure." He explained he had run into his landlady and the encounter had delayed him further.

I approached Thomas to confront him.

"Are you a relative of Charles?"

Thomas seemed almost hurt by the accusation.

"What?"

"You gave a false address to the club. 114 Elm Street does not exist."

"You are mistaken. It does exist. That is my mother's address in Chelsea. When I began here, I was living there."

I was taken aback by his quick reply. It did not seem to be a forced answer to cover a lie.

He walked to the middle of the room. "My dear fellows.

You suspect me of being involved with those rogues? Yes, I was excited when I thought the parchment was true, but weren't we all?" No one said a word, but everyone listened intently. "I suggest we do not point fingers. 'Two Tocks Before Midnight' it said. We have but thirty minutes to discover whether the whole message is nothing but a trick. Then, with clear minds, we shall discover who is behind all this business." He shook his head. "I assure you, it wasn't me."

Nearly everyone flooded to Thomas with the sincerest of apologies. I decided to wait until after midnight to offer mine. It was a clever retort, but I was yet to be convinced Thomas had no part in the affair.

"Everyone, listen," I said after giving Thomas a few minutes. "We have precious little time until midnight. We need to bar the door and stand clear from the window."

"Please excuse me for being rude," Thomas shouted, turning everyone's attention from me to him, "but after you falsely accused me of being a murderer, do you really think we should take orders from you? Lock the door, indeed, but what is with the window? Do you expect the angel of death to fly through on the stroke of midnight?"

He had moved in front of the window, taunting and strutting as a peacock for the attention of the others.

Thomas was emotionally upset—as would I, had I been accused of murder unjustly. But if he truly was the murderer, the truth had to be fleshed out before another could be killed.

I was preparing myself to explain our theory about the killer using a bow through the window when exactly the same occurred.

I can still recall the horror of that moment. Even now, it causes me to flinch. The shards of glass flew, but did no damage. The bolt, however, pierced Thomas' right arm, taking shirt cloth and skin alike until the projectile landed with a thud in the far wall. The collective gasps of the people in the room gave way to the sound of footfalls as everyone moved as far from the window as the room permitted.

Thomas dropped to the ground and I immediately rushed to him, keeping below the window. The wound, however superficial, was a testament to all that I had wrongly accused an innocent man.

Still, being near the window, I distinctly heard, from the outside, a piece of wood cracking and then a soft thud onto the street below.

"Listen!" I yelled, somewhat calming the commotion.

"I heard it too," said the captain. "Follow me."

Leaving others to attend to the stricken man, I pushed all emotions and bubbling guilt aside and rushed out the door, following Captain Barnwell and two police officers down the stairs. The killer was outside and a mere matter of seconds could mean his capture or escape.

Captain Barnwell held the lamp ahead of us, but even with the light we almost tripped over the body.

Joseph.

By the look of it, Joseph had taken the shot with the bow and had then fallen the two stories to his death. We found a crossbow, scattered bolts, and broken pieces of wood within a few feet from the body.

Looking up, we saw the balcony from the second floor had a missing railing. Joseph had simply applied too much of his heavy frame to it.

But something seemed off. It was curious in that I heard only a single crack of wood and a soft thud. I heard no scream. I saw no one pouring out from the building awakened by the noise. It was instantly apparent to me that something was wrong with the scene.

The captain, worked his lantern over the length of the corpse.

"Captain," I said, gaining his attention, "there remains one more. The third man. He most certainly is still in the vicinity."

"Quite right," Captain Barnwell said, kneeling beside the body and playing his clinical eyes over it in search of clues. "In that case, it may be better to search the area. You should return and leave the police work to us. It could be dangerous."

"If it is all the same with you," I said, revealing a pistol I had hidden inside my coat pocket, "I am very interested in what we find upstairs. I suspect we will discover the plot behind all these devilish deeds."

"I wouldn't think we will find much up there. Whoever the third man is wouldn't be so foolish as to stay at the exact spot of the crime."

"I'm not expecting a person, Captain. I'm expecting a candle."

"A candle, sir?"

I had caught the slightest whiff of melted wax and burnt wick. It brought to my memory an old time-delaying trick I'd learned during a brief stint in Europe.

The apartment building stood four stories high. The room we wanted was on the second floor. We woke the apartment manager and, after explaining our requirements, he quickly dressed himself and led us upstairs.

The room was let to an elderly woman who rarely left her apartment. Fearing the worst, the manager used his key after the third series of knocks.

Our fears were brutally justified.

"No doubt the old woman surprised the man as he was heading for the balcony."

"The men, you mean, Captain."

"The men, sir?"

"Shall we head to the balcony?" I said, not wanting to reveal my suspicions without further data.

The frail balcony door had been left open. We could see the broken railing and across the street, a perfect view of our meeting place.

"A moment, please," I said, borrowing the captain's lantern and kneeling at the balcony threshold. I examined the area, careful to illuminate every inch. The balcony was small; perhaps only two men standing shoulder to shoulder could fit.

As I suspected, there was indeed a hardened puddle of white wax in front of a knocked over piece of wood.

Carefully leaning over, I retrieved a small nail from the corner. Next, I rose and stepped out onto the balcony to examine the remnants of the railing. The wood was indeed old and weak, but not rotted. Far from being an accident, however, to me, the lone nail and the lack of rot indicated a saboteur.

Holding up the nail for the captain to take, I said, "If we find the boards downstairs with holes but no nails, we have 'men,' not 'man.'"

"The third man."

"Yes," I replied.

"But why?"

"Which 'why'? There is a big why and a small why. The big why, the reason for all this, is a mystery to me. But the small why, the reason for the unmanned launch, is to create an alibi."

"Do you suspect... Thomas?"

"I do, sir."

"Mr. Brooke, if you are correct and, I must say I believe you may very well be, you've made my job much easier. However, the law requires direct evidence. All we have is circumstantial." He paused before adding, "Are you in the mood for a spot of acting?"

"'All the world's a stage,' so sayeth the Bard. What do you have in mind?"

"Let's tell the truth... up to a point. I believe, there was a witness, wouldn't you agree?" said the captain with a wink.

"Quite."

❦ 6 ❧

Captain Barnwell and I returned to the group. He asked his two officers to fetch some materials from the department and wait outside the door.

Everyone was silent and seated, eager to hear our report. Thomas had a new smug look on his face. In retrospect, I believe it had always been there, but the new information had simply opened my eyes to it.

The captain raised his hands to gather the attention that was already his. My eyes fixed on Thomas throughout Captain Barnwell's speech.

"Joseph is dead. Mr. Brooke here has confirmed his identity."

My friends took a moment to let out a "thank God" or "a fitting ending to this horrible affair."

"Sirs, that is not all."

The men ceased their chatter and again gave the captain their undivided attention. Thomas remained the very definition of confidence.

"An elderly woman was killed tonight."

"By Joseph?" asked Christopher.

"Perhaps," the captain said with dramatic pause, "...or Joseph's murderer."

Expressions turned from a pitiful concern for the elderly woman to confusion. It was assumed by all that Joseph's death had been accidental. The nearly imperceptible smile that I alone had noticed on Thomas' lips disappeared.

"Joseph's murderer? Could this be the third man?" asked someone.

"That is our belief," answered the captain. "While we do not yet have the man's identity, we do have a witness."

I am sure the captain paused to allow me to closely examine Thomas' reaction to the word "witness." His face was stale, motionless. Had I not observed his earlier smugness, I would have had to say his face registered no reaction. But it did; I saw the slight change in his disposition. And with that change, I saw guilt.

The captain continued, "A neighbor saw a mustached stranger wearing a dark coat enter the room across the street," He pointed in the direction of the old woman's apartment. "She got a good look at the man's profile. The witness is in police custody and we will shortly have a drawing done revealing the murderer."

The chatter began anew. Thomas, the only man in the room with a mustache, stood and began moving toward the door.

"I'm terribly sorry," the captain said restraining Thomas with his arm but speaking to everyone, "but in the interest of your safety and police procedure, I must ask for each of you to remain here until the drawing can be completed. It is a dreadful inconvenience, but essential to our case. It is possible—indeed, probable—that one of you may know the man's identity and the whole matter will be brought to a happy conclusion tonight."

Thomas seemed to be on the verge of becoming belligerent, but after a moment, he reposed himself and returned to his seat next to the window without complaint.

"The department is a mere five-minute walk from here. The drawing should be here momentarily."

That is what he told our group, but in actuality, the captain had told his officers to wait outside for a full hour before entering with a satchel containing a blank sheet of drawing paper.

Minutes passed. Most members seemed to enjoy the waiting as if watching the lead-up to the climax of some exciting play.

And so it was—the captain's play.

Thomas, however, seemed more and more troubled. I no longer stared at him directly, but even a casual glance told me he understood the game we were playing.

The clock against the wall was near Thomas. Its tick-tock seemed to unnerve him more. Did its sound remind him of the two Tocks?

I will summarize that hour with the following description: most members were amiable despite having no knowledge of our drama. Toward the end, however, a few began to tire of conversation and wished to return home no matter the risk. Thomas took the opportunity to speak up.

"This is intolerable. You cannot keep us here like rats in some insane experiment," he said, standing.

"An interesting metaphor, Thomas," I said, seeing my opportunity. "An experiment expects some result. What kind of result do you expect?"

He was quiet. Sweat formed on his forehead, although it was not at all warm that October evening. There was no doubt then; he was guilty, and we had him.

"You are, of course, expecting your face on the paper."

"Oh, come now old boy," began one member in defense of

Thomas. "Do let's put all this aside. Haven't you had enough fun at Thomas' expense today?"

"But," the captain said, raising his hand effectively silencing the entire room. "What if the accusation is true? After all, he wears a mustache."

The room was ablaze with discussion, half of the room watched Thomas, the other half looked on me.

Thomas was shaking slightly when the knock to the door silenced the room once more. The officer walked in and after shooting a stern glance in Thomas' direction, he handed the satchel to the captain. The captain opened the bag and pulled the sheet of paper half-way out with an ostentatious display. With slow, deliberate motions, he returned the paper to the satchel, looked directly at Thomas, and cleared his throat.

"There can be little doubt, now." The captain's mustache remained motionless, forming the picture of a man with complete control of his being.

"There was no witness!" Thomas shouted.

"How could you know?" I retorted. "Unless, of course, you were there."

"I was here, you fool. I was here when the dart was shot, when Joseph fell to his death!"

"The dart, yes. Joseph's death, no," I said, taking a step toward Thomas.

"But Thomas was shot by an arrow," someone replied, rallying to Thomas' defense. "Someone who went to the trouble to create his own alibi would have no reason to risk being killed."

"Thomas is an expert marksman. He knew exactly where to stand in order to not hit his vital organs," I explained, keeping my eyes burning on Thomas. "But you were not intending to even graze yourself, were you? When you came inside around 11:30, there was no wind. I conferred with a policeman who had been stationed outside at the time. You aimed the crossbow precisely on target without correcting for wind. At 11:45 when the arrow was fired, however, there was a slight western wind, pulling the arrow to the left. You had intended it to come close, but not touch."

"But," someone else said, "how on earth could he have fired a crossbow across the street while physically standing here?"

"He used a candle as a fuse. He lit the candle shortly before 11:30. It burned for fifteen minutes at which point, the wick set off the main fuse which released a weight pulling the trigger. The kickback from the launched arrow pulled the last nail causing the already dead Joseph, crossbow, and rock to fall to the ground. With the poor light outside, the thread you used to tie the rock is practically invisible. Not knowing what to look for, the police wouldn't have bothered with one of a hundred rocks on the street. You intended to retrieve this on your way home, hadn't you?" I said, pulling out the rock and dangling it from a two-foot length of twine held by my fingers.

"But if he used a candle, surely we would have seen its light?" This time, Christopher spoke up.

"The crossbow was set on a piece of wood on the edge of the balcony. The candle was behind that wood, shielding its light from our view."

"You are insane," said Thomas in a fit of rage.

No one spoke in his defense.

"But the look of surprise on your face when the arrow flew into the window was not feigned," I said, addressing Thomas directly. "Oh, no. You were not expecting the shot so soon. Again, the wind worked against your wishes. Instead of twenty minutes, the candle, being fed extra airflow, burned the fuse in fewer than fifteen!"

All eyes were on Thomas who was now silent, clearly considering his options.

"I have to admit, it was ingenious," I continued in a softer tone. "Had I not witnessed a candle fuse before among miners in Southern France, I would have glossed over the slight remnants of wax on the balcony."

"You have no proof."

"Do you remember," I said, taking a step toward the murdering savage, "when Joseph returned to retrieve the parchment and we told him it was a forgery? We told Joseph nothing of our reasons. And yet, the parchment we found at the Chelsea museum corrected the Hebrew and stylistic issues. The exact issues we as a group spoke of only among ourselves."

"Surely Charles heard—"

"No," I said sternly, anticipating his words. "Charles was not there. He only returned to us this evening, hanging from a rope."

"You still have no proof," he said almost in a scream.

"We have a witness."

Thomas whipped out a pistol; I pulled out mine. The captain and the policeman beside him also had their service pistols drawn. The other members huddled, gasping at the unexpected development.

"But I must ask," I said as calmly as possible. "Why all this? What purpose did all these deaths serve?" Memory recalls my voice much steadier than how it really was.

Thomas kept silent but his gun remained steady.

"There was money at stake, of course, but there was something else, wasn't there? Something personal," I said, trying to read meaning from his expression.

"Who was Joseph?" asked the captain.

"You don't know by now?" Thomas answered, anger clear in his intonation. "Charles Tock's half-brother of course. He was an idiot, but Charles pampered him to his own hurt, blinded by some sense of loyalty to the dumb beast."

Thomas became talkative.

"Come, let us sit down at the station and have a long talk," said Captain Barnwell, edging closer to the increasingly desperate man.

Thomas backed up against the window, shards of glass surely pricking his back.

"All right. I'm giving up," he said, showing the broadside of his gun. But just as he appeared to lower it, he threw the pistol with a great force across the room. Instinctively my eyes followed the flight of the pistol. Turning back to Thomas, I watched as he leapt out the broken window.

We all rushed to see him roll off an awning and fall into the street.

"Quick! Downstairs!"

The men followed the police downstairs, breathlessly expecting a fourth body for the night. But reaching the location mere seconds after Thomas had jumped, we found no body. Bits of bloodied glass and wood fragments lay scattered on the cobbles, but no Thomas.

The street, at that time, was poorly lit. Even with the lantern the captain carried, the fiend had ample shadows in which to hide. We scoured the neighborhood but found... nothing.

$$\text{❦}\quad 7 \quad\text{❧}$$

I n the morning's light, minute trails of blood led us to believe our fugitive had entered the apartment building across from our meeting hall. Somehow, the bloodied mess of a man had crept inside while we were all flying down the stairs.

A door to door search revealed his hiding place. By morning, he had vanished, but the occupant, a middle-aged woman living alone, was tied and gagged. We had expected the worst, but he had left her alive. She had watched, bound, as he mended his wounds and left before the sun broke through the mist.

NEITHER THE POLICE NOR THE *AGORA SOCIETY* EVER FOUND Thomas. The search for the missing killer would remain a pet project that would pester Captain Barnwell until the day he died some ten years ago.

But stranger still, every year, on October 24th, I have, without fail, received a curious card in my mailbox. The card always arrived with but one word on it.

The first year—the first anniversary—I received the card, it read, "Tick." I discarded it as some nonsensical childish prank without even considering the date. However, the second year, the card read, "Tock," and I was terrified. Of all the *Agora* members, I had been most integral in discovering Thomas' hand in the matter. Captain Barnwell had a man stay at my house for the following week.

Of course, nothing ever happened. Except for the card alternating between "Tick" and "Tock" every year, I never saw or heard from Thomas again.

A few times I stayed vigil all night watching for him to insert the card. I learned he used delivery boys to leave the cards, never exposing himself directly. I always interrogated the boys—a different one each year—but they all said the same thing: the benefactor was a stranger. A tall man with a scarred face. And they were all paid handsomely for the delivery. Investigating the location the boys gave presented no clues and no Thomas. Ever.

The cards came religiously every year on October 24th. Every year until last year... It now being November of the following year, I feel that I truly am the last of the *Agora Society*.

THE MYSTERY HAS ONLY RECENTLY BEEN MADE MANIFEST. Shortly after writing the above, a woman named Lottie Phillips visited me in my lodgings. In her mid-thirties, she was a charming woman, well-spoken and regally dressed. She presented to me a letter sealed and addressed with my name, care of the *Agora Society*.

She discovered the letter after her father's death. Being curious, she traveled from Georgia to deliver it herself, hoping to learn something of her father's mysterious past. The contents of the letter revealed her to be Thomas

Phillips' daughter. I then realized that Thomas had taken his wife down south to hide from the law. As befitting a lady of honor, she did not open the letter nor did she demand I read the contents aloud.

THE LETTER READS AS FOLLOWS:

MY DEAR CARL,

By receipt of this post, you have evidence that Thomas Phillips is dead. What I did after the Agora Society is irrelevant and by offering you this information, I only ask you not disturb my family.

I became acquainted with Charles through the bank of my employment. And from that acquaintance, I was introduced to the Agora Society, his brother Joseph, and most importantly his daughter Carolyn.

I soon discovered Joseph's lust for money. Charles's brother was stupid and a petty thief, but I must admit, the forgeries were his idea. Upon seeing the blank parchments that Charles had acquired during one of his travels, Joseph asked of their value and from there the idea of the Book of Jasher forgeries was born.

We began work on our scheme a full year before the events of that horrid October. To keep our secret intact, Charles and I rarely spoke to each other at the Agora and never spoke of our families or social activities.

Emotional attachments are so often the downfall of great enterprises and so it was with ours.

I asked Charles for his daughter's hand in marriage. Carolyn and I had already pledged our love and needed only her father's permission.

But it was not to be.

He was furious and resolute against the idea of giving his daughter to a criminal as he called me. He would have broken off all contact with me had we not had the shared guilt of the forgeries together.

A few months later, Carolyn and I secretly eloped and moved across town. I still kept residence at my old place to receive visitors and of course to meet with Charles and Joseph, but at night, I flew to Carolyn. Her father, who did not know her whereabouts, was distraught.

We planned to move to a new town and leave it all behind, eventually sending Charles a letter explaining our marriage. I even gave notice to the bank. During that time, we were careful not to expose our location to anyone who knew her father. I double-backed and made false turns to thwart onlookers from learning of our location. Carolyn even wore heavy scarves around her head as disguise.

But Joseph found us.

He threatened to tell Charles of our marriage and to tell Carolyn about our nefarious activities—the facts of which she was never made privy.

Charles of course was in despair. He had no idea what had become of Carolyn and assumed the worst. He contacted the police and posted bulletins describing her appearance. Charles then quit the Agora Society *and plunged completely into what he was best at: creating the forgeries. And so, the three of us, encouraged by Charles' determination, redoubled our efforts.*

Again, it was Joseph's idea to approach the Agora Society *in hopes the experts there would certify the authenticity of the parchment. Such an endorsement would surely have enabled us to fetch ten times the amount we were seeking.*

The Book of Jasher *became Charles' sole reason for living. If you remember that night he appeared with the parchment, his nervousness prevented him from going back to hear your conclusion.*

As you so keenly surmised, I instructed them according to the points you made clear and, together, the three of us created and sold corrected parchments for a tidy profit.

If it were not for your insistence, our little endeavor would have succeeded without harm. But after reading your advertisement, Charles felt we could not continue. While strong in intellectual matters, he was exceedingly weak in will.

One day, standing before Joseph and me, he declared his intent to confess the whole matter. Clearly, this was not acceptable to Joseph or myself. To have such a blight against my name was unthinkable. For Joseph, the reasons were purely financial.

We tried to stop Charles, but he was most insistent.

It was Joseph's idea to kill his relative and to have the body discovered at the Agora Society. *I argued against it, but Joseph again threatened to reveal our activities to Carolyn if I didn't go along. I relented after devising a way to rid myself of both Tocks so Carolyn and I could begin our marriage properly. It required both Joseph's strength and... his death.*

It turned out the Agora *for the location was a good idea—and would have worked, I am sure, had you not been there. Joseph would be a natural suspect among any of you. Hence, the decision to stage the hanging at the* Agora *was perfect. When Joseph, the perceived murderer, died attempting to murder me, no one with any knowledge of our activities would remain alive. And with me being among the victims, no one would suspect me of the crime.*

At least, that was my plan.

But back to that night.

The fool Charles had fled to the Agora Society *no doubt with a mind to confess to you all that evening. For us, to find him outside the doors waiting for you to open it, was fortuitous.*

Of course, I had made a copy of the key from when I was on key duty and had easy access to the room. From there, with big Joseph's help, it was an easy matter to subdue and hang Charles.

You may wonder about Joseph. He was indeed Charles' half-brother, but with Charles threatening to end the easy income, jealousy overruled reason. Charles was the favored child—for his well-formed brain and the fact that Joseph was born a bastard. Joseph hated his brother with passion and only tolerated him thus far for his money-

making potential. With that gone, Joseph preferred to see Charles dead. Dead men can name no names.

Regarding this, I was in happy agreement with Joseph, but Joseph likewise, had too much knowledge of our enterprise. More importantly, there was the matter of blackmail.

While Joseph did much of the work as I commanded, he did not know the end of my plot. He asked why the candles. I softly replied, "You'll see." But now I realize I had lied. He never would see.

You may wonder why I have not sought revenge against you. After all, you are responsible for me losing a great deal of money. I should also mention the fact that you are responsible for the deaths of three persons.

In truth, I had intended to seek revenge, slowly. I wanted the "Tick Tock" letters to strike fear into you before I pounced. I planned an elaborate setup far more advanced than that of October 24th, 1859. But as time passed, my passion ebbed, my business increased, and most importantly, Carolyn and I had a child. Eventually, I lost all interest in the matter. I did continue the yearly cards out of tradition and nostalgia, however. I do hope you enjoyed my efforts.

You may further wonder why I write this. I shall never post this letter while alive, but in lieu of a confession, this enables me to offer you—should you outlive me—a more complete account of that evening.

YOUR OBEDIENT SERVANT,
    TP

—

HAVING NO HAND OR KNOWLEDGE IN THE AFFAIRS OF HER father, I felt it best to let Lottie Phillips live her life without knowing her father's darker side. I told her nothing of the contents of the letter, but spent the time, instead, telling her stories of her father before that dreadful night, before he murdered her grandfather and uncle.

After she left, I realized Thomas had given his daughter a name cognate with "Charles" as well as my name, "Carl." Lottie is a pet form of Charlotte, which is also related to *churl*. I spent that night in thought. Was the name given out of respect or guilt? Perhaps some attempt at penitence? Or was it simple coincidence?

SO THERE, THE MATTER IS RESOLVED, AND THE WORLD HAS the full story. Having only learned much of it recently myself, I feel somewhat relieved, completed.

Ironically, although Thomas had intended to tear the *Agora Society* apart, his actions had quite the opposite effect. We gained some measure of fame due to the incident, and many of our members went on to great worldly success.

The redoubtable Captain Barnwell often visited as a welcomed guest. He would present particularly troublesome cases for the club to consider, and, as a group, our members became closer than family.

With respect to our society, Thomas failed completely. But regarding his motivation behind it all, Carolyn, he most definitely succeeded.

Love can lead some men to greatness, others to their downfall. They say love triumphs over evil, but for Thomas, it only amplified the darkness that lay within him. Lies. Jealousy. Death. This was the legacy of Thomas and his "*Two Tocks Before Midnight*," the first great case of the *Agora Society*.

VOLUME 2: THE PENITENT THIEF

The Agora Mystery Series

❧ I ☙

February 14th, 1890
Carl Brooke
Boston

PRIOR TO PENNING THIS MISSIVE, I HAD NO INTENTION OF spilling any more ink chronicling the history of our *Agora Society*. However, to my shock—and I must admit, my immense pleasure—I received numerous letters of encouragement to divulge more of its secrets. It seems, the *Agora's* long and colorful history still holds interest even in these modern times.

While I had been willing to take the *Agora Society's* past experiences with me to the grave, I now realize what a disservice this would have been to the record of history. Yes, the *Agora Society* should be remembered and, as I am the sole survivor, it is incumbent upon me to share some form of accurate and in-depth knowledge on the subject.

So, with the full acceptance of this burden, I shall, to the best of my abilities, recount in a series of letters, the more remarkable cases and events in which the *Society* was a major player.

In the last letter, entitled *Two Tocks before Midnight,* I wrote of the downfall of Charles Tock and Thomas Phillips. Regarding these men, I have nothing more to report.

I was not surprised to discover that many of the letters I received after publishing the earlier tale seemed to be most interested in our encounters with the police, especially in form of one Captain Scott F. Barnwell. Indeed, during the course of our association, the steadfast captain and I became close friends. I do have much to share regarding our collaboration—this current letter only touching on it—but if I could write about only one other event from our society's long and colorful history, it would be with regard to the Penitent Thief.

2

L ate one evening, shortly after the War Between the States, Captain Barnwell arrived at my lodgings late, long after I had retired for the night.

"Mr. Brooke, are you in?"

The familiar voice did little to rouse me from my slumber, so deep my fatigue and pleasant the warm bed. This was followed, however, by an insistent knocking on my door. I woke to a half stupor, still certain the sounds were the last throes of an unsteady dream. But as I readjusted my pillow and allowed my eyelids to droop once more, the man shouted again.

In those days, I lived in a Brownstone that housed some twenty families. Fearing the disturbance would awaken the other tenants, I hastily heaved my second-floor bedroom window open and, poking my head outside, I saw the captain standing beneath a street lamp. With a wave of my hand, I made my presence known.

"Yes, Captain Barnwell," I said as softly as I thought my voice would carry without further disturbing the other tenants.

"Very sorry to bother you," he said, his voice matching mine in volume, "but it is a matter of some urgency."

I nodded and after a, "I shan't be a moment," I closed the window and dressed quickly. It was very much unlike Captain Barnwell to come calling after sundown, let alone so close to midnight.

Once I made my way downstairs and then out the door, my friend bombarded me with the most peculiar request.

"Mr. Brooke, would you mind coming to the station? Rutherford Nordlinger has... murdered someone."

"Nordlinger? The thief?"

"Yes, sir, the same."

"If you told me he had returned to thieving, I would have a hard time believing that, but murder?"

"The evidence is certain."

"And he has confessed as such?"

"He says he will make his confession only to you."

Only to me?

I was more than a little puzzled. Several years before, I had been of some assistance to Captain Barnwell in his search for and subsequent arrest of the man. As serious an offender as Nordlinger had been, he became just as serious when transforming himself into a pillar of the community. He served his time in the state penitentiary and made a great effort to right his wrongs—even going as far as paying double the amount he took from his unwilling victims. At Nordlinger's request, I oversaw much of the distribution of money. Witnessing this change of heart personally, I believed him to be truly a reformed man.

The last I had heard of him, before the captain wakened me, Nordlinger had joined a monastery, forsaking all worldly desires. By nature, I am skeptical of sudden conversions, but in Nordlinger's case, I had become convinced it was genuine. Even those he had stolen from extolled the new man.

"And this certain evidence?" I asked the captain as I popped my head inside to grab my hat.

"He was caught fleeing from the scene of the crime. His fists and sackcloth, bloodied. Let's go."

"Sackcloth?" I said, following my tall friend to the street and then to a brougham.

"Yes, he had become something of an ascetic hermit. Clearly all for show."

The captain barked his orders to the white-hatted driver and then nimbly leapt into the carriage. I climbed in beside him, albeit with less vigor.

The brougham lurched forward, hooves clattering on the cobble stones. The staccato urgency conveyed by the striking of iron upon street and the familiar rumbling drone of the wheels worked in concert with this shocking news to unsettle me completely.

Nine years of show... I was not at all convinced that Nordlinger was capable of murder even after the captain enumerated the seemingly clear evidence. He had been—as far as I knew—without fault for nine years. Why would he suddenly commit a murder?

As we turned round the bend of the street and met the fleeting light of a corner street lamp, I surveyed the dark silhouette of the forward-facing captain next to me. His brow, furrowed; his mustache firm. Captain Barnwell was never a man to express uninhibited emotion, but this utterly stoic disposition seemed quite unlike my friend. It told me his conclusion of the matter held no doubt.

"Is this the first you've heard of him in recent years?" I asked, raising my voice over the clatter.

"There have been at least two peculiar robberies in the past month. In each instance, only one thing of value was taken—something Nordlinger the thief was fond of doing—and both left a note. A third note, strikingly similar to the other two, was found on the body of the deceased this very night."

The cabby leaned to his left, pulling on the rein as he did so. As we turned a corner, a crisp night breeze splashed my face, awakening me to a point in the captain's words.

"A note? Stealing one valuable item is certainly reminiscent of Nordlinger's past modus operandi, but a note? I cannot think of an instance of the old Nordlinger doing such a thing. What did these letters contain?"

"Both were simply signed, 'The Penitent Thief.'"

My hands instinctively gripped my knees and I bowed my head to the carriage floor. It was pure shock, those words. Over the clap-clap of the single horse strutting upon the cobble stones, I told the captain what Nordlinger said to me while paying his debt to society. The thief's tone of voice and pained facial expression had seared the words into my memory. He said he felt a camaraderie with the Penitent Thief on the cross next to Christ's. I didn't believe him then, but in subsequent years, he proved his sincerity to me and to many others. And yet, upon hearing the contents of that note and seeing the look of utter conviction upon the captain's face, there seemed to be little doubt the man had returned to his old tricks. But if that were so, why would he ask for me?

"And the murdered man, who was he?" I asked.

"A Mr. William Ferris, by the card in his pocket. The corpse wore fairly shabby clothing—once a fine coat jacket now threadbare and dirtied. He had carried a bottle of whiskey in his pocket and a few coins. Nothing else. We are still investigating who he was and where he lived."

"Has Nordlinger admitted to knowing Mr. Ferris?"

"When we questioned the murderer, we had not discovered the dead man's name, but Nordlinger swore he didn't know."

During the short ride to the jail, I became convinced of

Nordlinger's guilt. The blood on his fists and clothes, recent thefts reminiscent of his past transgressions, and most pertinent to my mind, the note. The note was unusual in itself, but not the words: Penitent Thief, the very same phrase he had so long ago spoken to me in solemn oath. Despite such a weight of circumstantial evidence, one question continued to occupy my thoughts: why would he call me? I would be the one most likely to see him hanged for betraying my trust, the most sacred promise he gave me.

Captain Barnwell ushered me through the Charles Street Jail where Nordlinger was to be kept until his arraignment. The entrance opened into an octagonal rotunda with a tall atrium allowing in some of the splendid August moonlight. We entered a small hallway leading to a room with two chairs facing a window with stout iron bars. A minute later, two uniformed men escorted Nordlinger in to the room. He still wore his sackcloth. I engaged my old nemesis through the bars.

"Who was he?" I asked the moment he was seated. "A Jealous husband?"

One of my great personal faults, I freely confess, has always been my tendency to dispense with introductions or pleasantries when emotionally charged.

"I've renounced worldly pleasures, Mr. Brooke."

"Pleasures, yes, but not murder, I see. Were you looking for the most displeasing act imaginable and your mind came upon murder?"

"I am innocent of this murder, Mr. Brooke."

Captain Barnwell said, "Now see here, Nordlinger. You were caught fleeing from that dead man's body seconds after killing him."

"I was told to go there in writing. While waiting, someone hit me across the back of the head. When I came to, there was the dead man not twelve inches from my eyes. I swear by all that is good, I had no hand in this."

"But your hands had his blood on them," the captain said.

"I awoke with my hand on his bloodied head." Nordlinger turned his attention to me. "Someone wants me brought down by this."

"And this someone is not the only one," I said. The last time I saw him, I swore I would hunt him down should he renege on his promise.

"Mr. Brooke, I am guilty of many things. The more penitence I seek, the more wrongs I discover from my past and, most frighteningly, from my present. But this, I did not do. I would never take a man's life, sir. Life is sacred."

Captain Barnwell placed three pieces of paper in front of Nordlinger.

"What's this?"

"Your letters, perhaps?"

"The... Penitent Thief?"

"The very words you said to me when you left prison, Mr. Nordlinger."

"But... I did not write these letters. To whom were they addressed?"

I clearly remember Nordlinger's look of utter confusion. He was clever, I had thought. Clever and a great actor.

"In the homes of the recent burglaries."

"Burglaries?"

The captain's fist slammed down on the table in front of the thief. The boom echoed off the brickwork and reverberated through the confines of the room. Mr. Nordlinger jerked his head back in response to this sudden violent act.

"No more games! The monastery's records have you leaving three times in the past month and three times only. The first two were exactly the time of a theft. The last was tonight and that ended in a murder. Now, I've done as I have promised. I've brought you Mr. Brooke. Now honor your word. Make your confession!"

"I said I would tell Mr. Brooke the truth and I aim to do just that. I swear to the good Lord above I had no hand in this."

I studied the man's fearful face. Deep lines scored his forehead above raised eyebrows. Sweat beaded and then fell from a bald head down over his cheeks. Lips shuddered as if trying to coax words out of his dry throat. Voiceless tremblings. His eyes fell to his hands that rested uneasily on the table as though examining them for remaining traces of his victim's blood. The blood had been wiped clean upon arrival at the jail, but for a few heavy moments, he continued his inspection.

Returning his eyes to my face, he said, "It is true, I left three times but each time, I arrived at the location to find no one... The first two times, I simply returned home to the monastery. Tonight, I found myself attacked and upon waking... Please, Mr. Brooke, discover who has done this to me."

He let out tears that appeared genuine.

"Why did you ask for me?"

"Because, in you, I know there is an honesty which most of humanity lacks. You once helped me do right to those I wronged. Please."

"That will be quite enough—"

"Forgive me, captain," I said, curious as to what could possibly be Nordlinger's defense. "You said, you were told to go to that location tonight. By whom and for what purpose?"

"I received three letters from a man I had stolen from over a decade ago. Mr. Phillip Strauss was his name. He lived on Elm Street. I had forgotten the incident, but somehow the man found out and demanded I meet him to make restitution. As you are both well aware, it has been my solemn duty for the past few years to right all my past wrongs. I was compelled to go—even if it was impossible to confess this particular wrong."

"And you have no idea what it was that you stole from this man?"

"No, I... can't remember."

"What do you mean? You do admit stealing from the man, correct?" More than a trace of anger flowed from the captain's words.

"I believe so. It would have been in an area I frequented, but I honestly have no recollection of the event to which Mr. Strauss referred."

"And yet, you went not once, but thrice at the man's command," I said watching his reaction closely.

"As I have said, I took a sacred oath to repay everyone I have wronged. That of course even includes wrongs I may have forgotten. I have done much evil, Mr. Brooke. I have much of which to repent. You of all people know this to be the truth. I do not think it unlikely this was one of them." Nordlinger paused a moment before asking, "Tell me, who was the dead man?"

"You did not recognize him?"

"No, sir. This I swear."

I nodded to the captain who then said, "We believe his name is Mr. William Ferris."

I studied Nordlinger's face for some sign of deceit or surprise but saw nothing. I then stood. "If you are telling the truth, someone has gone to extraordinary measures to implicate you. Who could that be? Who are your enemies?"

"I... I can think of none. Please," he pleaded. "Help me."

I retained a stern appearance, but deep inside, my thoughts ran uncontrolled. It was certainly possible someone from his past would wish to see him locked up for life. In his darker days, he had been a drunk, a fighter, and of course a thief.

"I will consider it. Where are the three letters from Mr. Strauss?" I asked.

"Placed within the pages of my Bible in my cell. The head of the monastery will surely allow you entrance."

Without taking leave of the sorrowful man, I nodded and left with the captain following close behind. Once we had returned to the rotunda, Captain Barnwell asked, "What do you mean you 'will consider it'? The man is as guilty as the devil."

"The devil's guilt is evident in every inch of the world, within all humanity. Evidence of Mr. Nordlinger's current guilt is less clear. I dare say almost non-existent."

"But he left the monastery exactly at the times of the crimes and only at the times of the crimes."

"Doesn't that seem overly convenient? Would not an experienced thief such as Nordlinger be less obvious?"

"And he was seen moving away from the dead body."

"But not seen in the act. Also convenient, do you not think?"

The captain stopped me and stood in front with his mouth agape.

"You believe the man innocent!"

"I did not say that. At this junction, there is a greater than fifty percent chance the man is guilty. His past crimes and their similitude to the current events cannot be easily dismissed. However, if he is innocent, it means we are dealing with someone quite familiar with the old Nordlinger and someone who has a great desire to see him hanged. He is, after all, a man with much history, someone easy to frame. I would like to visit his home, the monastery in the morning. Would you care to join me?"

"The man is guilty."

"*Vincit omnia veritas*—truth conquers all. If he is guilty, let us prove it beyond all reasonable doubt and sleep well at night. However if there is but the slightest chance the man is telling the truth, it is our duty to find that truth. I could not live with myself if I didn't."

"All very true, but I'm afraid I will be busy with Nordlinger's arraignment in the morning. Please do come by the station should you learn something at the monastery."

I shook the captain's hand and left with great hope I might resume my quiet night's sleep at home.

※ 3 ※

The following morning, I traveled to the monastery located south of the city, near Mount Hope Cemetery. The quiet serenity of Boston's environs highlighted a delightful contrast to the mass bustle of the city proper. The sounds of birds and sweet smelling jasmine filled my senses with a satisfaction one rarely finds in the crowded metropolis. Sighing contently, I had my cabby wait for my return, and I walked through the entrance.

I was received by a chamberlain, but before announcing my presence, I spent a few quiet moments observing him leisurely tending to the grounds. His careful raking of the pebbled garden made my heart ache for the secluded and simple life. His ancient, bony hands worked deftly to create order out of the random pile of pebbles. Order out of chaos. Ah, the freedom to read, learn, pray...

In recent years, having long retired from public and private service, I have often reminisced upon that gardener and the peaceful thoughts that scene from so long ago brought to mind.

I watched him unseen from the corner for some time

before I shook my mind free of thoughts of books and quiet meditations and announced my presence.

Upon hearing the purpose of my visit, the gardener shuffled away to call the abbot.

A short time later, the abbot appeared wearing a simple brown tunic. The hood was pulled back to show a ribbon of gray hair encircling his bald pate. The fellow had no need to create a tonsure, however, the Good Lord having given him a natural start to his monastic career. The chamberlain whispered something to him and his previously peaceful eyes turned stern and suspicious, spilling distrust.

"Are you with the police?"

"I am here at the behest of Mr. Nordlinger with the agreement of the police, but I am a private citizen, an acquaintance, you might say, of Mr. Nordlinger."

"Tell me. Do you believe Brother Nordlinger to be innocent?"

"I cannot say."

"You do not wish to say."

"In all honesty, I believe he is more than likely guilty, but I would reserve judgment until after investigating the facts, which is the purpose of my visit. With your permission, I would like to examine his cell."

"Do you have a warrant?"

"No, I am simply here in an informal capacity."

"Then I must refuse."

"It will only take..."

"I'm sorry, but we are quite strict with our rules. Outsiders are not permitted within the living quarters unless extraordinary circumstances demand it. You may return with a warrant."

"Are these not extraordinary circumstances, Abbot? A murder has been committed."

The abbot remained firm in his silence.

"I see. A pity. However, I did receive a personal request from Brother Nordlinger. His Bible. His one request is to find comfort in its pages."

The abbot paused before acquiescing. "Very well. Wait here."

Five minutes later, I left the monastery and boarded the cab with Nordlinger's Bible in hand. Once out of sight of the abbot, I eagerly thumbed through the pages. As Nordlinger informed me, I found three small letters folded and placed in the early chapters of Jeremiah—the weeping prophet.

Careful to keep the Bible and letters from falling during the rough carriage ride—the roads were atrocious in those days—I examined them with care. The three letters came from the same stock of stationary, exceedingly well made. I was later able to compare the letters Nordlinger received with the papers at the scene of the crimes—that on which "The Penitent Thief" had been written. They were all the same stock. All six papers were a composite of hemp and esparto grass—old-fashioned and of exceptional quality. It was a fine paper, marking the owner as having considerable pride and station.

The handwriting was fluid, beautifully done. A quick comparison from Nordlinger's notes in the ledger of his Bible told me the letters could not have been his creation. As a youth, the man had lacked the opportunity to acquire a proper education. In later years, of course, he had read much, becoming a greatly educated man despite his youthful idleness. Still, the writing habits from his past carried into adulthood.

There were a few curious comparisons, however. Both had the tendency to flourish their capitals; both wrote with an open "a." While I am by no means a professional graphologist, the similarities, while stark, were not enough to make up for the differences in other areas. Indeed, the style between the two was so vastly different, I could only conclude without a shade of doubt the letters must have been written by someone other than Mr. Nordlinger.

Once my thought processes had led to a satisfactory conclusion, I had the driver alter course for Elm Street. Mr. Phillip Strauss, the purported author of the three letters, would be my next avenue of inquiry.

Elm Street, while once respectable, represented one of the poorer corners of the city. It consisted of a series of once radiant dwellings now dulled by neglect and the passing of time, perennially sad as if in mourning for the loss of better days. The building in which Mr. Phillip Strauss resided seemed to exemplify this condition most fully.

Upon arrival, I was accosted by several youths in dire need of a bath. I imagined they had in mind to offer their services to help my aged body alight from the cab or to try to sell me some trinket, but I preemptively quelled their entrepreneurial spirit by offering each, instead, a few pennies for sweets—or perhaps a bar of soap.

Once again instructing my driver to be patient until my return, I drew up beside a staircase and took a moment to observe my surroundings. I recognized the building from my research on Boston's architectural history.

As evidenced by the date carved into the keystone above the doorway, it had been constructed some forty years before during the Greek Revival period of Boston architecture. If I recall correctly, the owner, Charles Sears went bust during the Panic of 1837, and the city bought it for public housing. Its former glory forgotten, the condition quickly deteriorated to its present state.

Mr. Strauss answered my knocking without delay. Within the doorframe of his apartment stood a dilapidated man, a perfect fit for a dilapidated building. Early fifties, but his sullen eyes looked as though they had seen many years more.

The man with the sad eyes invited me in without hesitation. Before long, I determined that the purpose of my visit held no interest for him; it was only that I was a visitor. He seemed pleased to talk to anyone and by the opened locket he kept by his well-used Morris chair, I knew why. The inside of the locket kept a faded photograph of a beautiful woman forever frozen in youth.

"My condolences, sir. Your wife, I presume."

"Yes," he said, with some hesitancy. His shoulders slumped as he spoke and a nervous hand ran through his thin hair. I inferred that his demeanor, one of embarrassment, came from having left the locket in plain view.

Mr. Strauss motioned for me to sit on a couch as he made his way to the Morris chair. He picked up the locket and staring at it, he continued, "She was the best thing that ever happened to me."

"Do you know the name... Nordlinger?"

His eyes stayed fixed on his wife.

"No. Can't say I do."

I heard no variance in his voice. He lovingly set the locket down, gripped the arms of the chair, and leaned forward; his dejected eyes locked on mine.

"Who is he?"

His voice was little more than a whisper.

"A man who fears he has done you wrong. He believes he may have stolen something from you. Perhaps, fifteen to twenty years ago. Were you then at this location?"

"Twenty years..." The man's eyes stared blankly. "Nothing's changed. I didn't have anything worth stealing then as now."

"Can you remember losing or misplacing anything of value?"

The man returned his eyes to his wife and I feared my interview would not reveal anything worthwhile. Then, his eyes brightened with a memory. A sad glow replaced the sad dejection.

"Ah, I do remember one strange event. My wife was with child. We had just moved here—about eighteen years earlier, I believe. Life and blessings seemed to abound in those days. We were poor as dirt, mind you, but we had everything else it seemed. No longer. Now I am bereaved of wife and child and I still call this my home." He paused but before falling completely into a memory, he snapped forward and said, "Anyway, one evening, we were met at the door by a stranger who was, quite frankly, drunk."

"And what went missing?"

"A doll."

"A doll? Rare or antique?"

"No. It was just a filthy old rag doll. It had been my wife's from her childhood and she insisted on keeping it for our child..."

"I see. And you believe this drunken man stole the doll?"

"Yes. Well, who knows, but my wife insisted it was him. For the next year, she looked for that drunkard. It was very important to her, you see. She had left the doll by the bedroom window near the crib and that evening after the man left, it was gone. She always insisted it was he who took it."

"Did you invite the man in?"

"No, sir. I told him to go away and quickly closed the door. We laughed about it and thought the incident nothing of importance until my wife realized the doll was missing. I can only think he or an associate of his broke in through the bedroom window that evening."

A neighbor some rooms down was shouting at her children. The walls in the apartment were thin, outside sounds came through with little distortion. I could only imagine the cacophony of noise from the street below that would easily mask any intruder prying open a window and entering.

"And nothing else was taken?"

The man shook his head and returned his gaze to his wife's photo.

"You've been most helpful, sir. Please remain seated. I shall see myself out."

$$\begin{array}{ccc} \text{\ss} & 4 & \text{\ss} \end{array}$$

I left to meet Captain Barnwell at the station. It was, by that time, late in the afternoon, and he was eager that we should return to the Charles Street Jail.

Nordlinger's pale face and red-rimmed eyes indicated a man who had not slept since our last meeting.

"Who is she?" I asked as I handed Nordlinger his Bible.

He looked at me with raised eyebrows and trembling lips.

"The woman who wrote the three letters—as well as the three notes left at the scene of the crimes."

"Sir, the letters I received were all addressed as being from a Mr. Phillip Strauss," Nordlinger replied.

"The author of all the letters is a singular woman."

"How can you be so sure?" The captain asked.

I pulled the first letter that had originally sent Nordlinger out of his seclusion.

"Notice the flowing, Italian hand, the romantic and sentimental long finish of the gangling letters. Such ornate chirography is indicative of a female author. Handwriting is a gesture of the soul, my good fellows. These strokes are soft and free-flowing—beautiful and replete with significance and meaning. Feminine. It is voiceless speaking. Just as by voice we can infer personality, temperament, and mental and bodily health, we can do likewise with writing." I paused to observe both men's reactions. "I can continue. The gentle hooks at the ends of the letters a, t, and n are open. Quite feminine. The quill was lightly pressed to the paper. A man would press harder. The smooth strokes and slight flourishes on all the tailed letters. It is unmistakable."

The captain was not willing to allow the pendulum to swing too far into the realm of innocence. "Misdirection." He looked at Nordlinger while pointing to the letters on the table. "This man has cleverly disguised his handwriting to make these. It was all designed to throw us off."

"Impossible. I have seen Mr. Nordlinger's natural hand-writing. He is not capable of performing such artistry." I turned to the man and said, "I mean no insult. I only wish to establish relevant facts."

Nordlinger nodded uneasily.

"Perhaps, then, his wife?" asked the captain.

"Mr. Strauss'? Dead at least a year ago, and by the state of his apartment, there appears to be no other woman in his life. But more so than that. The man is penniless. The stationary suggests the author to be of some wealth."

"Then who wrote the notes?" Nordlinger's voice sounded confused but slightly hopeful.

"Someone who wanted to hurt you; someone who knew of your methods and where you conducted your crimes. You need to think who was with you then that knew of your methods. Someone who would now wish to betray you."

He shook his head in contemplation and asked, "Tell me, what was stolen from Mr. Strauss?"

"That is the most curious aspect. A rag doll of no value."

Nordlinger's eyes drifted into empty space. His lips began to stammer, his arms shake. "No, it..."

"Mr. Nordlinger?" the captain said, concern overtaking his usually stern appearance.

"I did it," he said without hesitation.

"Did what?"

"The thefts. I stole the dolls. I... I even committed the murder. I did it."

"Swear upon your Bible, sir," I said, pointing to the book on the table.

"I did it."

"Swear it!" I moved the Bible in front of Nordlinger's shaking hands and pounded my own fists on the table.

"I cannot."

"You will lie to me, but not to God. Why? Who wrote these letters? Who killed Mr. William Ferris?"

His voice was that of a mouse. "I did."

"No! A woman with some money and detailed knowledge of your past wrote the letters and devised this plan. Who is she?"

"I cannot, will not say."

"You will say or else you will bear the guilt for that man's blood."

He was silent. I crossed my arms and took a deep breath before continuing.

"I am convinced you had no hand in this, but if you do not speak up, you will have to confess this murder not only before a human judge, but to the Judge of Eternity! Speak."

"Joanne," he sobbed. "My poor little Joanne."

"Your daughter?"

"Yes."

It took a few minutes of sobbing and reflection before he grew calm enough to speak rationally. He then confessed how he had used his adolescent daughter to enter homes while he distracted the owners. How he taught her to steal and lie at an early age. How his wife's sister, Anne Walther, had taken

Joanne away while he was in prison. He hadn't seen or heard from his daughter since, but after his rehabilitation, he often tried to contact the sister-in-law to convince her to give him Joanne's location. She would not respond to his letters. When he made the thirty-mile trip to her house, she would only scream at him and remind him of his many sins. She finally told him Joanne was off studying in France but would tell him nothing more.

"You distracted Mr. Strauss while Joanne climbed the fire escape to the second floor, negotiated the parapet to her peril, entered their apartment, and stole the doll."

"Yes," he sobbed. "I... used my Joanne to her soul's hurt. Only a little girl would have seen value in a rag doll."

The pieces were falling into place. Nordlinger gave me the address of his sister-in-law and an idea how to procure a sample of her handwriting for comparison. I no longer remember the exact location, but it was a fairly well-to-do area not far outside Boston proper. I was to examine the handwriting sample and wait for Captain Barnwell there once he gathered his men. However, the result of her handwriting comparison made waiting a terribly hard thing for me to do. I had the last piece in hand; I simply could not resist finishing the puzzle myself.

§ 5 ₨

As I drew near the house, I marveled at its beauty. A bastion of classical glory, the two-story brick-clad Federal-style building stood perfectly symmetrical. An image of the geometrical ideal. The flat façade had two windows on either side of the door for each floor. Above the central entrance was a balcony supported by two stout wooden columns painted white and covered with stucco.

A lady opened the door mere inches, her right hand pressed against the frame as if to block even visual entry. Of her face, I could only see the left profile, but it was clear that she was impeccably dressed. Dark cloth flowed from her high neckline to her ankles. She wore perfectly white pearls on a necklace that contrasted well with the fabric. Her face—the half of which I could see—was stern and unforgiving. Pale as death, all her visible skin indicated someone who did not often step outside. But underneath the masquerade, I perceived she was concealing something, perhaps fear.

"I know you," she said immediately after I presented my name. "You are the one who helped Nordlinger appear honest enough to allow this current travesty to occur."

"You have marvelous calligraphy."

"Excuse me?"

"I had the opportunity to review a sample of it at the Boston Journal. You wrote a letter a few years ago arguing your own methods for reducing recidivism. I was particularly impressed by your passion if not your severity on the subject."

She continued to look at me indirectly, through her left eye. The perceived fear was still there. Her right hand slipped an inch.

"Go away."

"I cannot."

"I shall call the police and have them escort you out."

"I've saved you the bother. The captain of police and his men will be here shortly with a warrant to search the premises."

"I..."

In an instant, she jerked away the lily-white hand, and the door slammed shut. Although I hadn't seen anyone else, it was my impression that a man had ended our conversation by slamming the door. A few seconds later, shouts from inside confirmed it.

"Miss Walther!"

I pounded the door. The sound of shattering glass crashed through the wood. I pounded harder. The lady screamed, and I drew my revolver. Twisting the door handle, I shouldered my way in and saw a man's coattails fluttering around a corner staircase.

To my immediate left on the floor, Anne Walther attempted to push herself up to her knees. I fell to her side.

"I wanted..." I pulled a handkerchief from my pocket to wipe a jot of blood from her lips. "I just wanted him gone."

I nodded. Seeing she would be fine, my attention moved to the immediate danger. The killer.

"Stay here. Captain Barnwell and his men will arrive shortly. He will tend to your wounds and you will tell him everything."

I checked my revolver and took a quick look around the staircase. I saw no one. The killer had raced upstairs.

"The back," Anne Walther said.

I turned to the injured lady on the floor.

"There is an outside staircase accessible from the second floor," she added, pointing to the back of the house.

I nodded and made my way in that direction through an undecorated hallway leading to a nondescript rear door. The ornate exterior provided a remarkable contrast to the bare and neglected interior. Through a frosted window, I could see nothing but still shadows. Then one of the larger shadows moved. The killer. I ran to throw the door open.

A large man wearing a rather poor looking coat and tattered pants ran at top speed toward a copse of fir trees. Beyond that lay a thick forest, his intended course of escape. The man held a rifle in his right hand.

"Halt! Or I will shoot," I yelled, raising my pistol.

The large man slowed and stopped. He was easily forty feet from the nearest cover.

"Slowly turn around and drop your weapon."

"You ain't safe," he shouted still facing the fir trees. "She's lying."

"Turn around slowly."

He obeyed my instructions while lowering the rifle. At first, I felt relief. The whole matter was coming to a close and without further harm. Then, my fears returned in an instant. He brought the rifle to his shoulder in a swift motion. I leapt behind a large oak as a bullet slammed into the side of the house, an inch to the right of the doorframe.

My heart raced, but the man, however, was a terrible shot. The trajectory would have missed me by a good six feet even if I had stood still, but now, of course, I know he had not been aiming for me. Someone had been in the doorframe—someone I had not noticed.

The man was once again fleeing toward the trees at a manic rate.

"Stop!"

I took off after him with my gun at the ready.

He turned and aimed the rifle in my general direction. I had no tree to hide behind as before. Certain he meant to fire and left with little choice, I raised the revolver and pulled the trigger. The gunshot echoed as if I had fired twice. His rifle flew to his left. His shoulder twisted inward and hit the ground, quickly followed by the rest of his body.

A bitter tang lingered in my mouth. My chest heaved and burned. I took shaky breathes and fixed my attention upon the man whom I had shot—a motionless figure on the ground.

I closed the twenty feet in what seemed to be a single stride. There was no doubt. The man was dead. The bullet went through the heart, blood soaking the dry earth.

I turned back to the house. Anne Walther stood in the doorway, tall and self-assured, a totally opposite picture from a minute before. I blinked to confirm what I saw. She was holding a rifle of her own.

"He's dead," I shouted between heavy breaths. "You can lower your weapon."

"Thank you," she shouted back. She wore a curious smile as if the events of the past few moments had been exceedingly pleasing. "You don't know how much of a nightmare the past few weeks have been."

I stood and, with a heavy heart at the death of a stranger, trudged back toward the house, toward the woman who continued to hold the rifle at her side.

"He made me do despicable things. He was a brute."

"He won't hurt you anymore, but you must also clear your brother-in-law's name."

"Even if he didn't kill that man, Rutherford was quite guilty nonetheless."

The hand gripping her weapon tightened.

"Drop the weapon." I adjusted my grip on the revolver.

"He is a despicable thing, our Mr. Rutherford. My sister was too good for him."

"Drop the weapon," I repeated.

"That man! He's alive!" Her eyes bulged, and I took the bait, turning to see the man I had just shot remain still as death.

The report from her rifle hurt my ears more than my stomach, at least at first. I found myself on the ground not quite sure what had happened. Then the pain in my abdomen registered with a sudden ferocity.

"I do thank you," I remember her saying while walking toward me as I squirmed in the dirt, my weapon just out of reach. "With this fool here dead." She pointed the tip of her rifle at the dead man. "And you about to be, I have the perfect cover story. The captain will be quite interested in hearing all about Rutherford's intrigue with this riffraff." She kicked my revolver away before I could regain focus.

She then took a step toward me but was careful to stay beyond my reach. It wouldn't have mattered. The pain made the slightest movement nearly impossible.

"So," she said raising the barrel of the rifle to my head, "Good bye."

"Wait! I..."

A gunshot echoed through the trees. Crows flew. I awaited the impact, for the blackness of death, but... I continued to breath, continued to exist. Through blurred vision, I witnessed the woman fall. Beyond her, the now opened space revealed the uniformed figure of Captain Barn-well and his men...as darkness...closed around me.

❧ 6 ❧

The nurses at the St. John's hospital were top-notch, giving me both excellent care and company. The bullet had missed major arteries, but I required surgery and two months of bed rest to recover.

A day after the emergency surgery, Captain Barnwell and Rutherford Nordlinger came to pay me a visit. Nordlinger appeared with grateful tears glistening in his eyes. The Captain, ever stoic, smiled slightly as he patted my foot on the bed and gave me a, "Well done."

"I killed a man," I whispered, surprised by the weakness in those words.

The captain's mustache twitched. "No, Carl, you didn't." He took my hand and squeezed. "You nicked his right leg, but it was Anne Walther's bullet that silenced his heart."

I sighed in great relief. The mere idea I had killed a man —even in self-defense—kindled an agony within my soul, analogous to the physical pain of that bullet but with far greater implications.

Patting my hand and standing, the captain returned his

expression to his standard, sober form. With a nod, he repeated in a matter-of-fact tone, "Well done."

Rutherford seized my hand and expressed himself with greater emotion.

"I had no idea Anne was capable of such evil. She hated me, yes, and her hatred grew through the years, but murder?"

I swallowed and squeezed his hand as best as I could in my weakened state. "I'm very glad you kept your promise to me."

"Always, my friend. And," said Nordlinger with a great smile on his face, "with the good captain's assistance, we have discovered where my beloved daughter is. We found a receipt for a boarding school in Quebec. Much closer than France! The captain cabled the school and confirmed she is indeed a student there."

"You will go see her?" I asked.

A shadow fell on Nordlinger's face and he removed his hand momentarily. "I... My sister-in-law told her many things about me and, of course, the true things she knows about me will surely have painted me as a monster in her mind. Regardless, I cannot afford a trip and I am torn what to write in a telegram."

I smiled. "I have been thinking of taking a trip up north. Then, perhaps if the abbot will permit you a leave of absence, we can make the trip together, that is, if I ever get out of this hospital. Perhaps you will allow me to give you a proper introduction."

⚜ 7 ⚜

The abbot did sanction the trip and our *Society* saw fit to sponsor our journey monetarily. The first few minutes of the father-daughter reunion was a delicate matter, but upon seeing her father's tears rolling down his utterly sober face, Joanne melted into his arms.

She remained in Quebec to finish her schooling, which the *Society* gladly sponsored, but as often as possible, she visited her father in Boston. Their relationship blossomed and, after graduation, she returned and found work at a local bank in order to be near her father. I have since lost track of the girl, but at her father's funeral, she told me how grateful she was for the years I had given her with him.

Then she told me something that shocked me to my core. The one loose end, the one piece of the puzzle yet unexplained: who was the murdered man, William Ferris? Who was he and why had he been killed?

I had always assumed it was simply an act of convenience, an unlucky soul who happened to be available to make the frame complete. But some years earlier, her father had told

Joanne the man's name. She recoiled and explained that Mr. Ferris had once been Aunt Anne's beau. With his death, the evil woman had intended to remove two problems at once.

Mr. Ferris had come from a good family and had been quite wealthy. The match was promising for both families, but he had developed a gambling problem and a few years after they met, it sank him into penury. Before Anne Walther carted Joanne to boarding school, Mr. Ferris had often come calling, begging for forgiveness and money. She remembered her aunt shouting threats from behind the door. Mr. Ferris' visits continued, and she had taken on a personal bodyguard, the man I had most unfortunately shot and she had killed. By framing Nordlinger, she clearly intended to wipe away two undesirables from her past.

On a brighter note, Nordlinger formed a quick and lasting bond with Mr. Phillip Strauss, the man from whom the rag doll had been stolen. They met consistently until Mr. Strauss' death a few years later.

It is said the angels rejoice at the salvation of one man. At Nordlinger's funeral some twenty years after his prison sentence ended, the entire city—so it seemed—showed up to pay its respects. After reconciling with his daughter, he spent his remaining years building a group of concerned citizens— including an ever-interesting mix of ex-cons and monks— dedicated to the task of teaching respect for human dignity and respect for private property. While never formally incorporated, he often referred to it as The Penitent Thieves Society.

He was a good man and is greatly missed by those he touched and saved.

So, I end this second *Agora* letter. While far from dazzling with intrigue and criminal investigation, it was to me the most consequential of all cases. Rutherford Nordlinger became closer to me than a brother—always there for support. Oh, how I miss our deep discussions on the Holy Writ or even the particulars of some mundane current event. Despite his underprivileged upbringing, he was indeed a deep thinker. Sincere penitence created in him a most brilliant and compassionate man.

VOLUME 3: THE PEACE PARTY MASSACRE

The Agora Mystery Series

❧ I ❧

March 26th, 1890
Carl Brooke
Boston

I have no keener pleasure than to read the swelling influx of letters that seems to grow each day. As mentioned in the last letter, I am quite taken aback by the interest shown in our *Agora Society*. There have even been demands to recharter! While I am not averse to such a proposal, at my advanced age, it is beyond my power to do any such thing. The requests, however, do fill my chest with a great sense of pride.

Regarding the so-called *Peace Party Massacre*, I have two motivations for speaking on the subject.

First, I wish it to serve as a sort of introduction to the figure who looms so vividly in my nightmares, Thomas Drake. Many sensational reports have spread afar regarding the evil he has wrought upon this earth. I will not deny the most sensational of them—indeed, I will confirm and expand upon the popular imagination! Never have I experienced a greater

83

heartbreak and loss than that suffered at the hand of Tom Drake. With the greatest respect to Johnson and Webster, no written definition can truly capture the meaning of a word behind an emotional impulse; experience, and experience alone is the source dictionary for such feelings. Through Drake's tutelage, I learned the true meaning of the word "hate."

Undoubtedly, many will know of what I speak, to wit, his connection with my wife's passing. I must beg the reader's patience yet a little more with a solemn promise of a future explanation. The scene, too vivid. The pain, too fresh for current elucidation. However, regarding our society's first introduction to him, the matter was not personal, and I could not have foreseen its final consequence.

My second motivation for speaking on the subject is to give honor to our friends in Wilmington, North Carolina. Much has been said—or rather, whispered—regarding the Peace Party members, and it is my desire to tell their story from within the context of the time and our Society's direct involvement.

Therefore, I give you this third letter entitled, *The Peace Party Massacre*.

🦋 2 🐚

I t was after the war and as our club endeavored to give aid to our fellow men, we eagerly agreed to help to rebuild Wilmington's economy. We also had a mind to aid freedmen find honest employment.

Our *Agora* had had a special relationship with a Society in Wilmington called *Nec Temere*—at least we had a relationship before the war. The name was a shortened form of the familiar Latin phrase, *"Nec Temere, Nec Timide"*—meaning, "Neither rashly nor timidly."

Most of the military action during the war was far from Wilmington proper, but its industry had been devastated and the unserviceable Wilmington Port was in dire need of repairs. Our main objective—before subsequent events rendered it subsidiary—was to tend to these needs.

Scott Lords, the engineer behind the Clarkesville Dam, was present to lend his expertise. With his knowledge and the club's name and resources, we had planned to hire freedmen and dock workers to get the port operational within a month.

Little did we know, the form of our help would soon turn from an engineering task to one more forensic in nature.

It was a dark and terrifying time. Some disenfranchised Confederate soldiers who had come of age through blood and war found it difficult to pick up a hoe and accept the inevitable. Some turned to crime. One such example is featured in our present letter, the aforementioned Thomas Drake.

But I must return to the general circumstances before delving into the specifics.

During the long years of the war, all contact between the *Agora* and *Nec Temere* had been lost. As their name might suggest, the near unanimous opinion during those dark days —we later learned—was an "honorable peace." That is, most members wished to preserve the antebellum status quo, avoiding war in order to continue daily business. These were the men of the so-called "Peace Party" of North Carolina.

These men were certainly not pro-slavery. No, the evil that was slavery had to be dealt with—they were all in unanimous agreement. However, the belief that the matter could be settled only by secession or war was openly questioned by the Peace Party members.

This, as you may imagine, did not sit well with their more headstrong neighbors. These people saw a different form of slavery with Washington as their overlord. The Peace Party members were, in their eyes, little more than traitors and collaborators.

Shortly after hostilities ceased, our *Agora* members were greatly thrilled to receive a letter from the president of the *Nec Temere* society. We had been, after all, enemies even as we were true friends and fellow countrymen. In their missive, we were told, they had certain needs, particularly regarding the port. An opened port would enable trade to enliven the local economy and speed recovery. They expressed their hope that we would be in the position to send some aid. Three of us—including myself—made the trip with a substantial monetary donation from our group.

Our names were:

The professor of Theology, John Hitch, the engineer, Scott Lords, and the present writer, Carl Brooke.

I can be quite certain about the accuracy of much of what I will now recount. As a matter of policy, all members out on club business were required to keep a detailed journal of all that occurred, not only expenses, but also, a timeline of events. I still have my notes and will refer to them to clarify and enhance my aged memory.

❧ 3 ☙

I n those days, immediately after the war, there was no direct link to our destination by railway. To give an outline of our odyssey, we travelled as far south as track would permit and hired a carriage for the remainder. The roads being in such disorder, our progress was unbearably slow and oft delayed. Those two days of arduous travel, today, would be accomplished in a few hours.

A cluster of street lamps extended its light up a gentle slope, leading to a series of two-storied buildings. We made our way to the one that matched the address given in our invitation letter, and arrived at the *Nec Temere* meeting hall late one evening. They had offered to open the meeting hall for our accommodation and we gladly accepted their hospitality. Not knowing the exact date of our arrival, one club member was assigned to wait each night in the event we made our appearance. The man on duty the night we arrived happened to be the club president, Mr. Jonas Tobias.

A minute after engaging the metal knocker, the door opened to a middle-aged man with sleep-laden eyes. The poor roads and unexpected engagements in Boston had delayed our departure, making us later than we would have been and I'm afraid we had caught Mr. Tobias napping.

The eyes squinted further as he adjusted them to the dim light. He disappeared momentarily and returned holding an outstretched candlestick. The farsighted man held the fire so close, it nearly set our faces ablaze.

None of us had known Mr. Tobias before this meeting, but once fully awake and with his glasses on, we found him to be of the most agreeable character. We were soon seated around a polished oak table and, after the required salutations and refreshments, his face turned serious as he shared with us grave and unexpected news.

"We had requested your humanitarian aid and we truly are in great need, but I'm afraid we may have a greater urgency regarding your more... colorful services." Mr. Tobias readjusted his legs as he leaned into our circle. "The matter with Mr. Tock and your many subsequent adventures aiding Captain Barnwell is well known even here."

We looked on silently, listening with increasing interest.

"You see, last week one of our own, Mr. Jacob Sanders, was gone missing. His wife, Carol, came to us last Thursday during our weekly meeting asking if we knew what had become of him. She was beset with tears and simply impossible to console. We, of course, did not know of his whereabouts, but we comforted her as best as we could and implored her to wait at home in the event he should return."

"How many days, at that point, had he been missing?" I asked as the hurried Mr. Tobias paused for a breath.

"According to his wife, he left the house Wednesday morning as usual but has not returned since."

"A full week has passed, then."

"That is correct, sir."

"And of the local law enforcement?" John asked. "What has been their response?"

"I'm afraid, that has been a bit of a problem. The sheriff is full of patronizing talk, but weak on action. Should you gentlemen have a desire to help us in this regard, we shall go to the sheriff in the morning and you shall see what sort of fellow he is."

After a silent meeting of our eyes, the three of us agreed to accept the case at once.

"Of course, Mr. Tobias," said Scott. "We should only be too happy to offer our services—however humble they may be."

"Oh, blessed day—those simple words alone will have a steadying effect on the nerves of all our members."

"But I must ask," I said quickly, wishing to rid of unpleasant questions first. "Has this Mr. Sanders been known to leave town without a word to family or friend?"

"No, sir. Never."

"I do ask your pardon for a second rough question, but can you think of any reason why he could have left on his own accord or as a result of his actions? Alcohol or debts?"

"Mr. Sanders is clean as clean and straight as straight. I can vouch for his integrity as sure as I am standing here today. He doesn't drink or gamble, and he adores his wife. I do not think him capable of the slightest indiscretion."

"With marital unhappiness precluded, we may have something more dastardly on our hands," Scott said, his bushy eyebrows forming a matted block beneath his curly dark hair. The youngest and one of the more animated of us, Scott leapt to his feet and said, "Do you think someone has done him harm?"

"That," said Tobias, "is precisely what I am afraid of. I must hasten to add one important piece of information. Mr. Sanders was an outspoken critic of the war before hostilities began. While he maintained a more circumspect attitude once war was inevitable, many of our citizens saw him in a most negative light."

"I see. I assume the sheriff would be one of those citizens," I said, speculatively.

"Among others." He gave a firm nod.

Mr. Tobias' eyes were still heavy with sleep and having unburdened himself from his great worry, his eyes looked to be ready to give in completely. I thanked him for his hospitality and suggested that he meet us around nine in the morning for our visit with the sheriff. With that, Mr. Tobias returned to his house and we retired to the clubroom, which had been thoughtfully furnished with several mattresses and amenities suitable to attend to the needs of weary travelers.

"I wonder what part the sheriff has to play in this," John said while pouring each of us a glass of water from a pitcher. "Mr. Tobias seemed quite reserved when discussing him."

Scott shook his head. "A terrible thing and for the local law enforcement to be so disinterested in the welfare of one of Wilmington's citizens. A shame."

Setting my empty glass aside, I said, "Let us not pass judgement on the sheriff just yet. We shall meet him tomorrow. Perhaps Mr. Tobias' distrust is quite unfounded."

Positioning a few blankets atop a reed mattress, I reclined and allowed my travel-wearied body to sink into a bed that seemed, to my fatigued mind, to be the most comfortable in the world. I had every intention of joining Scott and John as they continued their conversation into the night. That intention, however, would last but a few moments. With each breath I exhaled, sleep grew and my curiosity waned. Before long, I had drifted off into a sound and restful sleep.

$$ \text{❧} \quad 4 \quad \text{☙} $$

Our meeting with the sheriff the next morning did not go well.

A quick glance at my notes tells me I failed to record many particulars of that meeting—I didn't even write down the man's name. I believe I had been so incensed by his conduct I simply wanted to put the whole matter behind me. I well remember the sheriff making light of the President's recent murder. His crude quip sparked outrage within us all. We parted soon thereafter and with little affection for the man.

But with this sheriff being so integral to our present story, I will make use of the advantage of knowing the end of the matter to fill in the blanks accordingly.

That morning, we followed Mr. Tobias and his aide, Mr. Lee, to the sheriff's office.

While the sheriff's name escapes my memory, his appearance and general brutish mannerisms do not.

The large man received us while still seated with his feet propped up upon his desk. His insincere smile revealed a missing front tooth. His ears, gigantic and blood red, shot out of the side of his head not unlike those of a bat. Gray strokes of grizzled hair stuck out from the edges of his well-worn cap. He had a habit of thrusting his short, stumpy fingers out at the person with whom he was conversing. In short, his physical appearance, sound of voice, and content of conversation were an offense to my senses. Even so, he maintained an ever-present smile—a smile that only made him look rude.

"Mr. Tobias," the sheriff said, not dropping the crocodile smile for a moment. "What have you brought in? I do hope these aren't out-of-towners coming to stir up trouble."

"Sheriff, these gentlemen are here to help us find Mr. Sanders, and we were hoping that perhaps the good sheriff's office in Wilmington would have some information for us today."

"These investigations take time, boy," the sheriff said, waving his hand dismissively. "We don't want to rush things, now do we? I'm sure Sanders will show up one way or the other. Now, please, let law enforcement do its work and you go do ... whatever it is you do."

"Sheriff," I said, my voice causing a momentary ripple in the man's ever-present smile. "One would assume law enforcement would be grateful for any assistance when a prominent citizen such as Mr. Sanders has gone missing. And yet, you act—"

"Mr...?"

"Brooke. Carl Brooke, sir."

"Mr. Brooke, we don't take too kindly to outside interference. If you want to tell me what to do, I'd be obliged if you'd run for governor or at least mayor. Otherwise, good day."

The smile was gone and with a dismissive wave of the man's fat hand, the meeting was over.

Once outside, Mr. Tobias apologized profusely. He carried on to explain that the sheriff was under a great deal of stress and perhaps our being here was not as helpful as he hoped it might be.

"My good fellow, on the contrary," I said. "Our being here seems to be for a good reason. We will find your Mr. Sanders and see to it that the sheriff is shown the folly of his ways—if it is true that he has had no hand in this matter."

"Sir?"

"How long have you known the brutish fellow?" I asked.

"In point of fact, I have little knowledge of him. I, of course, have had some minor dealings with him on a fair number of occasions regarding business matters, but never socially." Tobias shook his head emphasizing a most unpleasant thought.

"What bothers me is when he said, 'Mr. Sanders will show up one way or another.' That may well indicate the sheriff somehow knows something, and his callous hospitality—or rather, *lack* of it—has only hardened my resolve to uncover this mystery."

A great look of concern overtook Mr. Tobias' face.

"Dear friends," he said, giving each of us a compassionate glance. "I do hope you will be careful. I believe the sheriff to be well-intended, but his methods have been known to cause incidental injury."

Tobias then went on to tell of an acquaintance of his who had been falsely accused of embezzling a large sum of money. Before his acquittal, he found himself with two broken bones and a number of written threats to his wellbeing. The sheriff, he emphasized, may not have been involved, but he was in charge of the matter and Tobias had had his suspicions.

"There are courts of law," said Scott, crossing his slender arms.

"Not in Wilmington, at least not since hostilities began. The war created a vacuum within the law, I'm afraid. I implored the man to seek a counselor-at-law from the state level, but even while nursing his broken bones, he denied the sheriff had borne any responsibility."

It did not take much to convince me and my companions the sheriff was a contemptible fellow. His attitude and potential past abuse of power made him quite suspect in this current case. But as to what connection he should have with the missing man, it was anyone's guess.

❦ 5 ❧

From the Sheriff's Office, we moved directly to Mr. Sanders' house, seeking a statement from the man's wife. It was a humble dwelling, comfortable and cozy but meager. The drawn blinds and dark stone lining gave the feel of a reclusive hideout.

The wife did not invite us in, but she did answer our questions hesitantly from behind the screen door, which she opened but a little. She swore she had no new information. There was, however, something in her mannerisms that alerted my suspicions.

Mrs. Sanders had a fidgety left hand that was constantly fingering a curious bird-shape pendant which hung around her neck on a length of fine chain. She bit her lip after answering each question and spoke without emotion, rarely even appearing saddened by the mention of her missing husband. She spoke of him in careful tones.

"I'm sorry," she said, "but I have no further information. Please talk with the sheriff. He has all the necessary details."

Again, the sheriff. Could his involvement be beyond a professional interest?

After she closed the door on us, Mr. Tobias wore a rather shocked expression.

"She had been so imploring and desirous of our help that night at the club meeting," he said once we had left the property grounds. "Most imploring."

"How well do you know Mrs. Sanders?"

"Not very, but Mr. Lee's wife is somewhat acquainted with her."

"Yes," said Mr. Lee who had maintained our company after the visit with the sheriff. "My wife has done nothing but speak of Mrs. Sanders' tragedy."

"I hate to mention a delicate subject," John asked, keen to help illuminate the situation, "but could you ask her if there was any indication Mrs. Sanders' relationship with her husband had turned sour?"

"I can answer that now. As I said, my wife has done nothing this past week but speak of the tragedy." Mr. Lee's eyes narrowed at those words. "She has repeatedly sworn that Mrs. Sanders is of the highest moral fiber and only two weeks ago was speaking of joining her husband on a second honeymoon of sorts in Raleigh."

"I see."

The woman who had answered the door seemed almost devoid of care—or at least more careful in speech than in heart.

"There was a hat. A man's hat—but it was no gentleman's hat—on the chair behind her. There is very little chance, then, she could be harboring a lover?"

Mr. Lee looked aghast and threw a hand to his vest. "Mr. Brooke, I do declare..."

I held up my hand. "I apologize, but you must admit, the woman we just met resembled someone who had something to hide."

"Yes," Mr. Tobias said with some heaviness. "Her mannerisms were rather queer, but to insinuate that..."

"Her ring," I said, interrupting the man's words.

"Sir?"

"Did you notice her ring? Or rather, the lack thereof? From the moment she opened the door, she had her left hand up and moving, waving in our faces. Impossible to miss. She wore no ring."

"Perhaps, she had no ring—the wedding band isn't a universal custom around here. And ... I hesitate to mention it, but due to the circumstances, I feel obligated to say that Mr. Sanders is one of our poorer members. During the hostilities, he lost his bee-keeping farm and his occasional work with a local printer became less in frequency. While he is a principled and honest worker, the scattered work he found could not cover his expenses entirely. Our club gifted Mr. Sanders a small stipend to help with his daily needs. He had—has—a brilliant mind, but currently of meager means."

"Even so, she wore a ring recently. The tan line proves it. Perhaps," I said with hesitation, "Perhaps there had been some debt. The ring has gone missing. That could be accounted for by a repayment of that debt."

Mr. Lee immediately spoke up. "Mr. Sanders was indeed a man of meager means, but a debtor, he was not. Each month, we would present him with a gift to help him with expected expenses, and at the end of each month, he would return to the penny any money left over. He kept a detailed tally of not only what we had given him, but of how every penny was spent. *Every penny.* If he had needed more money to cover additional debts, he would only have needed to come ask for it. As the club treasurer, I can confidently say Mr. Sanders is the most trustworthy man I know."

"Mr. Sanders ... There speaks the name of virtue," I said greatly affected by the man's actions. "It will at once be an honor and a pleasure to meet him."

But I was not entirely convinced of his wife's piety. Why was she so hesitant when speaking with us? What was the meaning of the missing ring? Even if it was for a repayment of debt and not some extramarital affair, would that yet show a basic contempt for her missing husband?

From that day, we took shifts secretly watching the front of the Sanders' house. The single post was sufficient—so we had thought—to gain a complete knowledge of the comings and goings of the house. A road leading to town ran directly in front of the house and in the back, stood a wall of dense forest, without an access road for miles. From our hidden location and with Scott's monocular, having been brought for surveying, it was an easy matter to observe all traffic. For the duration of our watch, not once did she leave the property, and no one came calling.

❧ 6 ❧

We did many things in the days that followed; none led to Mr. Sanders. We made daily contact with the sheriff. Each encounter was somehow more unpleasant and less revealing than the one before. Still, it showed him we would not give up and that we still held out hope for Mr. Sanders' safe return.

Then, one visit, I entered the sheriff's office alone, intent on forcing some cooperation from him, when I noticed a wadded-up paper in the trash basket.

I do not know why or how it sparked my interest. It, however, seemed somehow significant even though it was little more than a hunch. During my travels in the Orient, such a feeling was said to occur when one utilized the third eye. Whatever the source, there are undoubtedly moments in life beyond the rational or explainable. After all, the natural, not being able to create itself, had to have been caused by the supernatural and one would not be amiss to believe the effects of such a creation must still manifest itself through miracles or perhaps even through mild hunches. Whatever the cause, I knew that paper held great importance even if there was no rational reason for the knowledge.

"What do you want?" The sheriff was as tired of seeing me as I of him. He no longer bothered to show that unfaltering smile.

Upon seeing the paper, however, I instantly released any outward show of anger. I shrugged my shoulders and let my hands slip into my side pockets. My fingers fell upon the round shapes of a few loose coins and I came upon an idea for my next course of action.

"Perhaps, sir, you were right. We have been more of a nuisance than help, I'm afraid. I can only imagine how vexing our interference may have been for your office." I looked up and saw the smile had returned, albeit a smile mixed with confusion in his eyes. "You had every right to disdain our supposed help."

"Well, now, that's mighty kind of you. You do understand how delicate any police work can be, but a missing person's case—all the more so."

"Yes, indeed. Well, I just wanted to let you know we will be leaving shortly. I do have some local business to tend to, but once that is finished, we will head back north."

I pulled my right hand out to offer the man a parting handshake. A few coins dropped carelessly to the floor near and into the wastebasket in front of the desk.

"How clumsy of me," I said while bending over to collect my items.

"It does takes a big man to admit he was wrong," said the sheriff. I clearly remember the relief in his words. "I suppose, I should apologize for my earlier rough behavior."

"Not at all," I said after collecting my coins. "One can only ask for a sheriff to do his job."

I waited until I was halfway to the *Nec Temere* meeting hall before retrieving the sheriff's garbage from my pocket.

The hunch turned out to be a wanted poster. A crude sketch of a shabby-looking fellow had, above it, a headline: Thomas Drake

The identifying features followed. Most striking were two unmistakable points. The man had fiery red hair, and, on his arms, a series of tattoos of unusual symbols that marked the man as an unsociable fellow. He was said to be unevenly tempered and was to be considered dangerous. The offered reward was substantial and recently issued. This last fact made me wonder why the sheriff had discarded the poster.

At the moment, I still only had hopeful suspicions of the significance of my find. Why would the sheriff throw away a wanted poster? Had the criminal been apprehended so soon and if so, how did the sheriff learn of it so quickly? Or, perhaps, the sheriff did not wish this Mr. Drake found.

I went directly to Mr. Tobias who had graciously taken an

extended leave of absence from his work to tend to our needs. His eyes popped wide upon seeing the poster.

It soon became apparent that Tom Drake was well known in Wilmington.

Before reaching the age of majority, he had already killed two men. In subsequent years, his activities broadened into every criminal scheme imaginable. But most intriguing was the statement by one of the *Nec Temere* members that there were a number of Drakes in the sheriff's family.

I was no closer to discovering our missing Mr. Sanders, but I was now certain the sheriff held secret clues if not the outright answer.

Then, we had another breakthrough.

The same day we discovered the link between the sheriff and Tom Drake, Mrs. Sanders came to us in a most hysterical tenor. Her head was down, and one gloved hand covered a large portion of her face. Her other hand held a bulky knife, the tip of which was stained, dirtied by grime and what looked to be dried blood. I quickly retrieved the knife as it appeared it would soon fall from her shaking hands.

"Mr. Tobias, Mr. Brooke—you must forgive me. I lied to you." Her voice cracked, but she continued unabated. "I have some further knowledge regarding my husband's disappearance, but you must believe me when I say I withheld the information out of the belief that doing so would speed my husband's return."

John Hitch, who had been on watch at Mrs. Sanders' house, burst in. He had no doubt been following her as she left her home.

"Go on." I withheld any comments until hearing her statement in full. Still, at that moment my thoughts were crowded by the wasted time and resources caused by this woman's silence and misdirection.

"Good sirs," she said, removing her hand and lifting her

face slightly, "it was only this day that I learned how terribly, terribly deceived I had been."

Seeing her full face in the light, I rushed to Mrs. Sanders and examined her left eye, which was bruised and greatly swollen. "Quick," I said, snapping my fingers, "a towel and cool water."

"There is no need," she said between sobs. "This will heal, but I fear the pain I caused my dear husband will not."

I offered her a chair. She flopped down, consumed with misery.

My eyes fell to the knife still in my hand. Some etchings on the butt of the handle caught my eye. Tilting it into the light, I could clearly see the initials, "TD."

"Tom Drake," I said with little doubt.

"Yes." Looking up, her eyes betrayed a momentary veneer of surprise before they returned to the floor in a dull glaze. "He came to me a day after I told the club of Jacob's disappearance. He told me he had heard of certain bandits looking for my husband. Thomas relayed to me a story that Jacob had a secret gambling problem and through a series of considerable losses, he had a debt beyond his means and with the most unseemly of people. I, of course, did not believe him. The Jacob I knew would never even touch a pack of cards. But as time passed and it seemed Thomas' words were all anyone knew of my husband's disappearance, I wondered whether it could be true." She stopped, caught by tears that had somehow slipped from her eyes down to her throat.

Examining the knife's handle further, I saw a slight gap and what looked to be threading. I gave the top a twist and more threading appeared. A few more turns had the top of the handle completely removed, revealing a cavity in which some folded paper had been hidden.

"What's that?" asked Tobias

John, standing to my side, leaned in. As I tugged the

paper free from its hidden chamber, I noticed some other object deeper in the handle. Handing the paper to John, I tilted the knife down and a tiny jade amulet fell into my waiting hand.

I held the object up to the light. "A statue of a bird. A stylized bird somewhat reminiscent of an Egyptian god." I looked at Mrs. Sanders whose hand, once again, was gripping her necklace which also held a bird-shaped charm.

"It is a small page full of strange markings," said John, holding the paper for all to see. "Not quite Greek."

"No," I agreed. "Perhaps it is Coptic Egyptian?"

Mrs. Sanders let go of her bird-shaped necklace, her eyes wide and staring at the jade amulet in my hand.

"I," she started. "That's mine. Tom must have stolen it from the house."

"Yours?" I walked over and placed the miniature statue in Mrs. Sanders' hand.

She quickly slipped it into the inset pocket to the side of her dress and then, placing her hands in her lap, laced her shaking fingers.

She hung her head low and in a sobbing voice, said, "I'm quite fond of birds."

"About Tom." I handed her a handkerchief. She took it with an unsteady hand. "And what did he do next?

"Yes." She used the handkerchief to clear her tears away. "Thomas said he could find my dear Jacob and cause the debt to go away in its entirety, but only if I agreed to a few conditions."

"And these conditions?"

"That I give him my wedding band and tell no one of the gamblers or of him. He had been most insistent on the last point."

"Were you acquainted with Mr. Drake before this incident?"

She paused, looking intently to the floor as if the script for her next words would be found etched in the planks.

"Yes. We were childhood sweethearts you might say. But after ...well, he chose a path I could not follow."

"I see. And you let him stay at your house while he supposedly went out looking for your husband."

"Yes," she said, lifting her eyes to meet each of ours. "But you must believe me. He truly appeared concerned for my husband's wellbeing. And to me, he did nothing inappropriate, nor did he approach me in any unsavory way. That is, until today." She averted her eyes from ours once more. "He had a daily routine. He would appear early in the morning, sleep or eat all day, and then go back out after dark in search of poor Jacob, at least that was what he claimed to be doing."

We, who had spent the past week watching her house, looked at each other. Both the house and the only road accessible to the house had been monitored constantly.

"Can you tell us exactly how he left and returned to your house?"

"Through the basement hatch in the back. He would then exit to the nearby woods and hike to a connecting road some two miles away. He told me he kept his horse there."

We had indeed scouted the wooded area, but we had not ventured that far out. We had found no evidence of traffic—in particular, searching for that of horse traffic. We had simply assumed visitors would have to originate from the access road immediately in front of the house.

"When he came back each morning, what did he tell you?"

"Nothing. He wouldn't tell me anything. I entreated him with my tears every morning. But he would tell me nothing of my poor husband. And then this very morning he grabbed me and demanded that I leave my husband for him. Horrified, I pushed him away and ran to the door. He caught me before I could escape and then he struck me," she said, touching her wounded eye. "He said ... he confessed that he had taken my husband, but that confession was not with a contrite heart; it was almost as if he was prideful of his actions. He told me if I did not leave my husband for him immediately, he would kill Jacob. He told me a woman willing to remove her wedding band by request displayed contempt for her husband and that he would be a better man to me. I at once ran out the door screaming with shame and pure terror."

Her face burned red. She was now enraged.

"My nearest neighbor, dear Mr. Hoiser, heard the commotion and came directly to my aid. I grabbed Mr. Hoiser and told him to run get the sheriff. He pointed to his carriage that was saddled and readied. Just as I reached the horses, I heard an awful scream. I turned to see Mr. Hoiser on the ground with that knife in his back. I ... I don't know what I was thinking—perhaps my desire to defend myself from Thomas who was then running toward me—but I grabbed that knife... I pulled it from poor Mr. Hoiser's back and got on the carriage. I kept on until I arrived at the sheriff's."

"To the sheriff? What was his reaction?"

"To laugh at my hysterics. He said he had heard Thomas Drake was hanged in a county over. He suggested I had seen a ghost and that I should lie down a spell. He told me if I did not go straightaway to my house, that he would arrest me for public incitement."

"My dear lady, I fear this delay has cost your husband dearly. But by Tom Drake's actions, it does seem Mr. Sanders is still alive. There may be hope—but only if we leave without delay." I looked at the men around. "Quick. Everyone must be armed. Mrs. Sanders, please lead us to your home. I would like to see anything Mr. Drake left behind and then we shall begin the hunt."

We gathered nearly twenty men from the club and friends

who could be trusted. A search of Tom Drake's living quarters at the Sanders residence yielded nothing but the sheath for his knife. I mated it with the blade and kept it on my person. We fled to the basement and out the hatch, intent on tracing his nightly journeys. She pointed to the direction the rogue had taken each evening.

"Mrs. Sanders, it would prudent if you were to wait at the meeting hall."

I clearly remember her horrified face upon hearing those words. She had failed her husband and wanted nothing more than to put right her grievous error of judgment. There was no doubt in my mind this was her motivation.

Looking back these many years hence, I do wish I had argued with her more persuasively, but she was the most natural guide, and I was in total agreement that she did have an unfulfilled obligation to her endangered husband.

❧ 8 ❧

Nearly thirty minutes later, the dense wood gave way to a broad clearing, through the middle of which ran the road. We searched in the direction of the rising sun and, upon finding horse hoof tracks leading behind us, we faced our shadows and followed the path.

Although details become less clear as I age, I do remember my exhaustion at the time. My notes simply report it as a blisteringly hot day. The cool wooded area had kept our spirits up, but once we left the shade of the trees, the temperature quickly climbed. All of us were spent. We had taken eight-hour shifts, constantly watching for Tom Drake or any movement from the Sanders' house. The realization that all our day-long watches and late-night vigils had been in vain made the exhaustion all the more potent.

Still, we pushed on, keeping to the side of the road should we need to conceal ourselves quickly in the wood. The prospect of the discovery of Mr. Sanders kept our feet moving; the thought of an armed Thomas Drake kept our eyes vigilant. We were rewarded with the occasional horse hoof print here or there or other clear signs of someone else's recent presence. Tom Drake's presence. We had been sorely tried that day, but we were at the cusp of the truth.

Someone cursed in the distance and, in an instant, we scattered. We moved behind trees, shrubbery, or any other object large enough to hide a man, or in Mrs. Sanders' case, a woman.

Through the branches, I saw a figure on a horse emerging from the thicket. He moved from the dark wood to the road as if he had materialized out of the ether. Shocks of brilliantly red hair stuck out from under his hat. There was no doubt. It was Tom Drake looking uncannily like the drawing on the sheriff's trash: gruff, unkempt, and sorely angry.

He was alone and mounted, moving at a leisurely trot toward us. The grumbling and cursing grew louder as did his menacing figure. It seemed he was furious about something but, for the time being, oblivious to our presence. His capture was to be imminent; he was on a horse, but we were armed and had surprise and the numerical advantage.

We whispered a plan. Ambush. I insisted Mrs. Sanders stay behind us all. We were twenty men against one, but if he could get one shot out, it would undoubtedly be directed at her.

We waited until he was close. But before I gave the signal, his cursing stopped. He pulled off toward the woods and goaded the horse to full gallop.

"Tom Drake! Stop or I will shoot!"

I had my pistol at the ready, but the horse and its rider ignored my warning and were quickly moving out of range. I lifted and took aim.

"No!" It was Mrs. Sanders. She got up and began to run to me.

"Stop her!" I said, keeping my eyes fixed forward while restoring my aim, adding gradual pressure to the trigger to ease out the slack. Two men held her back. I squeezed.

In the distance, I saw a puff of red fly into the air above Tom's right shoulder. He was hit and wounded, but he managed to stay mounted and slip into the dark woods in the direction of the Sander's house.

"Mr. Tobias," I said, "take Mrs. Sanders and a few men to search for Mr. Sanders. The rest of you, follow me after the rogue."

I took off at once, unwilling to think of the implications of what had just transpired. Mrs. Sanders' actions had undoubtedly saved the life of her husband's kidnapper and even potential murderer. The wonder of it! We had lost our nearly perfect chance to catch our game.

Drake had entered the woods on the opposite side back toward the house. We'd lost sight of him, and without transportation matching the agility and swiftness of a horse, we decided to return to the house directly and search from there. There was a chance he would attempt to retrieve his belongings.

❧ 9 ❧

I was not present with Mr. Sanders' search party, but I carefully recorded what transpired in my logbook.

Following my commands, they entered the woods, looking for any tracks and following any trail the kidnapper might have used to get to Mr. Sanders. The trees were sparse enough to allow a rider passage, but the thickening wood soon made it obvious which paths were taken. Broken twigs, bent limbs, and the occasional hoof print in moist soil led them forward.

Finally, they heard a cry and moved swiftly toward the source of the noise. Tied to a large oak was Jacob Sanders, blindfolded and in an affront to all decency, completely unclothed.

As the party approached, his muscles occasionally twitched and shivered. There was very little skin without some bruise or cut. Later, we realized the cuts were actually intentional, made into strange symbols. Applied to much of his body was a thick substance which was soon revealed to be honey. Producing honey had been Mr. Sanders' principal occupation prior to the war and Thomas no doubt exploited that fact.

I am told Mr. Sanders heard the sound of Tobias, the two other men, and his wife and took them to be Tom returning, perhaps with a group of scoundrels to enjoy the spectacle.

For a moment, the rescuers could not speak. The shock of the sight made any word quite inappropriate. Then, the blindfolded man cried out loudly, piercing the hearts of his would-be saviors and most powerfully, the heart of his wife.

"Just kill me!"

Mrs. Sanders moved first, running to him sobbing and begging for forgiveness—of what, her husband had no comprehension. The confused and blindfolded man said nothing, clearly unsure of what was transpiring. She wrapped her arms around his sticky body and smothered the unseeing man with kisses. Tobias moved in to take away the blindfold and immediately commanded the other two to find a nearby body of water.

A stream was discovered not a hundred yards from the man's location. His legs having been bruised and mistreated required Mr. Sanders to be mostly carried. After removing the layers of honey and giving him a generous amount of water to drink, the three men each removed an article of clothing and soon had Mr. Sanders in a state of decency.

❧ 10 ❧

Meanwhile, as the rescue party began to make their way back to the house, we were searching the area at length for any sign of the madman.

Finding nothing even hinting of his presence, we posted guards around the perimeter of the house and the rest of us headed back to the woods to aid in the search.

We were soon united with Mr. Sanders and his rescuers.

I rushed over to relieve one of the two men supporting the pitiable man. As I neared and saw his features, I was filled with a certain horror. He was wearing one of his rescuers' shoes, pants, and his bare chest was covered by Mr. Tobias' fine frock coat. But his face ... Eyes clamped shut ... The surrounding flesh, swollen and discolored. Queer markings carved into his chest. He held his mouth open revealing several missing teeth. The man was hanging on to consciousness. Surely, a day more and the man would have perished.

From here, I shall include Mr. Sanders' own account of what happened up to his rescue. His own prose far exceeds any poor attempt of mine to imitate. The following letter was written many months after the incident and sent by courier to us in Boston. As you will surmise, Mr. Sanders never did discover his wife's history with the fiend—not totally, at least. It is of considerable relief to me that he finished his days with pleasant thoughts of his wife.

To the Esteemed Agora Society *of Boston Massachusetts:*

I shall forever be indebted to Mr. Brooke, Mr. Lords and their dear colleagues from the respected Agora Society *of Massachusetts.*

I left my wife that Wednesday with every intention of arriving at the printing house by eight-fifty in the morning as usual. But the curious paper that I before presented to Mr. Brooke and, as requested, reproduced below caused a delay to my usual habits.

I had received that letter the previous night. My wife had no knowledge of it—I had the intent to verify its contents before causing her undue pain. I now regret not sharing it with her. It would have no doubt brought the whole matter to a much happier and swifter conclusion.

The letter went as follows:

We demand that you print a broadsheet recounting the names of traitors belonging to your Peace Party to be published at your expense and advertised throughout our city and country. We feel it is only just for you to cover the costs considering the fact you have printed the bylines and treacherous articles of many of the names below. Traitors must be shown their error.

You have one day to comply.

[...He then listed several dozen names including that of myself and most members of *Nec Temere*...]

When the search party found me, I had been exposed to the elements for nearly two weeks. I had been clothed and somewhat cared for, given food and water at odd intervals during the night, but never during the day. I have no knowledge where the man left to. However, the morning I was discovered, something had befallen the kidnapper to greatly upset him. I know not what. Furious and raving mad was he. He spoke of killing me in a most unsavory way. He forced me to undress at gunpoint and tied me to the tree more thoroughly than before. Blindfolding me, I felt him use his knife on my chest; I bear its marks as scars to this day. As Mr. Brooke requested, I have reproduced the symbols faithfully below. Lastly, I felt honey pour over my body. He left mumbling his hope that some wild animal would not come before he had a chance to return for the ceremony. For what kind of ceremony, I haven't the faintest idea.

But I am alive thanks to the members of your society who so selflessly risked and nearly gave all to save me. I am forever in your debt.

I remain, your obedient servant,
Jacob Sanders

AS A MATTER OF CURIOSITY, I DID ASK MR. SANDERS MANY months after the incident to send me drawings of the symbols the fiend cut into his flesh. In addition, I received a copy of the strange paper I had found in Tom Drake's knife handle. It too had similar markings which were indeed related to the marks on Mr. Sanders' flesh. The reader must once again forgive me for not expounding my findings in this present letter; a discussion on the symbols and their meanings will be far better suited for when I speak once more—and finally— about Thomas Drake.

We took Mr. Sanders to his house and tended to his wounds as best we could. We tried to get him to go directly to the doctor, but he insisted on going to his house. We relented, but I had someone gallop to town to have the doctor come to him. His wife was constantly by his side, attending to his every need.

Once inside, he pointed to his writing desk and told us to retrieve the above-mentioned letter. Through labored breaths, he insisted we let him tell us of the hidden facts behind the matter. An idea latched itself to my mind.

"A curious message," I said, smiling at Mr. Sanders. "Mr. Tobias, would you be so good as to retrieve a blank piece of paper and a pen from the writing desk?"

I glanced at Mrs. Sanders while Tobias did as I asked. She was the picture of devotion. She was as devoted to her husband in that briefest of moments as any woman could be in a lifetime. I sighed as I put pen to paper.

Not wishing to lose the original evidence, I got to work creating a fine copy of the threatening letter. My chirography wasn't outstanding, but I was far from a novice.

Tobias, who had observed my peculiar look, said, "Mr. Brooke, how the devil are we to find the man?"

I smiled and held up the paper.

"The sheriff is related to Mr. Drake, is he not?"

"Yes. Distantly."

"He intentionally led us and other officers of the law away from Tom Drake."

"Yes. The man ought to be reported to his superiors. They'll get him to talk."

"Might we use an alternative form of persuasion? I say, let's engage the good sheriff's services. I wager he will be most motivated to find Tom Drake for us."

"Have him help us? And motivated to do so? Indeed!" Mr. Tobias said, a frown evincing his confusion.

"It has become apparent to me the man may treasure something more dear than kin." I stood and placed a firm

hand upon Mr. Tobias' shoulder, leading him to the doorway.
"If you would be so kind."

Tobias' carriage was still in front of Mr. Sanders' house.
We boarded and took off. Within thirty minutes we were near
the sheriff's office. I had Tobias stop and I dismounted,
taking Tom Drake's knife and the copy of the letter with me.

"Pull the carriage into this alley and wait. I shan't be but a
moment."

I was certain of the sheriff's ambitions and regard for his
own standing. Relations notwithstanding, he would do
nothing to jeopardize his station in life.

Turning the corner, I peered through the window. Inside,
the sheriff paced the small office. He clearly knew something
was amiss. I carefully maneuvered unseen around the window
and stopped at the door. No one else was around to witness
my secret act. I quietly placed the paper against the wood
and slammed the knife—Tom Drake's knife—through,
tacking it to the door with a solid thud.

At the bottom of the letter, I had written in blood red
ink, "Peace Party Massacre!" I admit it was theatrical and of
poor taste, but getting the sheriff's attention was paramount.

By the time the sheriff opened the door, I had fled around
the corner. I didn't risk peeking, but I am all but certain the
semi-permanent smile was gone.

"Okay, now we wait," I said to Tobias upon returning to
the carriage. "In a few minutes, I will report the disappearance of you and one or two others in the *Nec Temere*."

"Of me?"

"But of course. It would be a gross mishandling of justice
to not do so."

"A gross mishandling, sir?

"He may have been willing to cover up one kidnapping of
a man he had reason to dislike, but as sheriff he can't have a
maniac—no matter the association—running around kidnap-

ping and murdering citizens he was sworn to protect. My report will be corroborated by Mr. Drake's note. In addition to Mr. Sanders, your name and the names of several other prominent citizens have been crossed out on the copy attached to the sheriff's door."

Tobias nodded in understanding. "You think he will go directly to the fiend."

"If I am not very much deceived, the sheriff will be leaving quite soon thereafter and in an Almighty hurry."

A few minutes after I returned from reporting dear Mr. Tobias' disappearance, a horse galloped past the alley in the direction of the Sanders' house. The rider was none other than the heavyset sheriff.

"Quickly, as we can. Let us return to the Sanders' residence."

Mr. Tobias nodded and gave the horses a good whip. I closed my eyes allowing a rare moment of relaxation. It had been a trying week, but the end was in sight.

Or so I hoped.

⚜ 11 ⚛

"**N**ot so fast; not so close," I called. "It is all right if we lose track of him, Mr. Tobias. He will be going to Mr. Sanders' house first. When the sheriff learns Drake isn't there, I will take a single horse and follow him closely."

We arrived in time to see a horse aimlessly walking around, loose and behind the house. Beyond that the sheriff's horse was tied to a small tree. On the other side of that horse lay the prone body of the sheriff, shot through the head. The hatch to the basement was open. Drake, the killer, had clearly entered the house.

At first, my breath caught, believing several people to be in the house. Then, to my great relief, I saw Mr. and Mrs. Sanders and Mr. Lee outside the house hiding behind a line of bushes. Mr. Sanders, already in poor condition before this fright, had a utterly pale face. He lay against the trunk of a tree, his breathing labored. The doctor who had been called was there tending to him, but without medical provisions. No doubt, his bag, instruments, and medicine were inside the house.

"Tobias," I said to the man still seated in the carriage. "Head back to town. Gather any men willing. Tell them to be armed and ready."

Tobias stammered for a moment, seeming lost in indecision.

"Go!"

As Tobias did so, I began a jog out of an area of safety and toward the bushes where my friends were hiding. The jog became a sprint when I heard the report of a gunshot.

As I dove into the bushes, I saw a second gunshot had sent twigs and parts of leaves into the air not a foot from my head.

"Carl!" Scott said. Scott and John were flat to the ground.

"I'm fine," I said quickly before my mind would convince me otherwise. "What happened?"

Lee crawled to my position. "Everyone else went in all directions searching for Drake thirty minutes ago. We heard a gunshot, ran outside, and saw the body of the sheriff. We have to move Mr. Sanders. This last horror has hit him hard."

"Can anyone see the man now?" I asked.

Each member of our group replied in the negative.

"I can attempt to enter from the back," I said asked pointing to a series of thinly leafed trees that would provide cover: poor cover, but cover nonetheless.

I slowly rose, crouching to prepare for a sprint toward the first tree when Lee placed a heavy hand on my shoulder. "I tried that. The nearest cover is just too far. He's watching for any movement."

I nodded. A more direct approach would be needed then.

"Tom," I shouted. "Come out unarmed and ensure your hands are where we can see them. We have you surrounded. There are twenty of us." It was only half a lie; the other fifteen or so were miles away searching for the outlaw.

The response was instantaneous. "I've bettered worse odds."

Drake used the butt of his rifle to break the glass out of a window on the second floor. He shot several times in varying directions, hitting none, but using the violent act to look for movement. I urged for all to stay still as it appeared he wasn't certain of our numbers or all our locations.

The situation had not improved when, a few minutes later, several of the others returned. Another rifle shot informed them most directly of the grim circumstances. With my arms, I signaled Tom's location and instructed them to stay low.

As I spoke, Mrs. Sanders simply stood up and shouted toward the house. Her husband had been falling in and out of consciousness and needed immediate medical attention. The doctor could do nothing in the present situation, a fact that without doubt motivated Mrs. Sanders' actions. With the horse and road being guarded by Tom Drake's rifle, we feared to move him, but he needed to be transported as a matter of some urgency. Seeing his wife put herself in danger, he moaned, but no longer had the power to speak.

"Thomas. You had it all along." She pointed a defiant finger at him which soon formed itself into a wagging fist. "Your oaths mean nothing. Curses on you for breaking your vows." She spat on the ground. "Curses!"

After a few moments of silence, she stood straight, taller. I moved my hands down in rapid motions, trying to get her to fall back to the safety of the small hill behind which the rest of us hid. She ignored my frantic motions and took one more step forward.

"Answer me!" she shouted to the empty second-story window.

The response was a loud crashing of glass from that window. I watched as Mrs. Sanders faltered. As if to illustrate her commitment, however, she took yet another step toward her husband's kidnapper.

"Where is it?" cried a voice from behind the broken window.

I could not see her face, her back being to our group, but I noticed her hand touch the pocket in which she had placed the object from Tom's knife. I merely suspected then what I confirmed later; the bird figure played some devilish role in all this. Content, she then turned slowly and began to walk back us, to her husband. A quite out of place smile graced her face.

I remember her husband spoke at this point. "Carol," he said, "don't leave me." The man was exhausted and dehydrated, but he seemed to have some understanding of his surroundings.

I honestly do not remember hearing anything when the bullet flew from that window. I just looked up and saw Mrs. Sanders eyes grow suddenly wide and then her body fell with a sudden collapse.

How little we appreciate the fragility of life. A doctor can direct, but the body does the work of healing. A flash of potassium nitrate or a slash of a knife and it is gone.

I saw her face—unmoving. A wound spilled red life from her chest. I shook my head, heard myself scream, and took aim.

All together, we filled the room with dozens of rounds of lead. There could be little chance of Drake's survival and, with that thought, I led a cautious group toward the house to find the body. I knelt next to Mrs. Sanders. A quick feel of her carotid artery revealed no pulse.

The crashing of more glass sent us leaping for shelter, but this time, the shattering of glass was of some object inside and not a window. He had somehow survived the gunfire and had taken the house's lanterns and spilled the oil throughout the second floor. It took little time for the fire to become visible to us on the outside.

I ran in and up the stairs with my pistol drawn. I saw nothing but thick smoke and felt the heat from a nearby unseen but raging blaze.

I moved with haste to the basement and found the opened hatch which the murderer had so often used to escape the house. I completed a quick search of the room and, seeing no sign of Tom Drake, I exited and ran to the others, instructing them to search the woods and keep their weapons ready.

While the others hurried toward the woods, I stayed with Mr. Sanders who had somehow managed to crawl over to his wife's motionless body.

We watched as the conflagration reached its zenith. It became apparent that if Tom Drake had not escaped, he could not have survived. By our constant and thorough watch outside on all sides of the house, it was all but certain that Tom Drake was no more.

But leaving you, dear reader, with such an impression would be a lie. As many of you know and the stories testify, the murderer did indeed survive.

Once the fire was extinguished, we searched the remains thoroughly. We looked everywhere—everywhere except the compartment we later learned had hidden Mr. Drake. During his time there, Tom Drake discovered a concealed room in the basement. It had once been a wine cellar but had been converted to a vault to house honey. It was from this room that he had taken the honey and found the key to his survival.

Mrs. Sanders was dead. Mr. Sanders, incapacitated, was immediately taken to a hospital. No one remained who knew of the subterranean hideaway. And so, by our ignorance of the house, the vile murderer escaped.

Regarding Tom Drake ... as I previously mentioned, our

final meeting shall be recounted in a later letter. I will need time before putting this story to paper. He was an evil man, eager to take pleasure in other people's pain. I personally and uniquely share with Mr. Sanders evidence for the truth in this statement.

I will mention one minor fact irrelevant to this present story, but vital to understanding my final encounter with Drake.

The jade bird which I had discovered within the handle of his knife was gifted to our club in lieu of payment. We declined at first—oh, how I wish we had remained firm in our refusal!—but Tobias and the other *Nec Temere* members were insistent we should take the artifact. They were unsure of its origin or meaning but when Mr. Sanders verbalized his wish that it be gone, we gladly accepted the clearly ancient piece. John, in particular, was quite pleased with the matter, being interested in any object from Egyptian antiquity, as this object did appear to be.

But as for the matter of the *Peace Party Massacre*, once news of the story spread, Wilmington showed gracious courtesy toward Mr. Sanders and all those formally associated with the Peace Party. In a way, the kidnapping and murders aided reconstruction far more than our original plans could. It brought an end to the local discord.

Whilst we were unable to accomplish our original tasks, our actions only added to the Agora Society's reputation and esteem. This, I suppose, was our legacy, an act of heroism that fulfilled the Agora's charter by making the world a somewhat better place.

VOLUME 4: THE CURSE OF THE MAD SHEIK

The Agora Mystery Series

May 15, 1890
Carl Brooke
Boston

The many requests for a letter involving my friend Captain Barnwell continue to arrive in my letterbox with alarming frequency. I fear I have neglected the will of my readers and, to address this deficit, I shall spend the next two letters chronicling incidents in which the captain played a part.

I shall never forget a sad case that occurred some thirty years ago, a short time before the War Between the States. I present it here with the admittedly theatrical title, "*The Curse of the Mad Sheik.*"

IT BEGAN DURING ONE OF THOSE EVENINGS IN WHICH I found myself alone at the *Agora Society* meeting hall attending to club papers.

On that gloomy midsummer's evening, I had opened the

windows in vain hope of a breeze. To aid circulation, I also left the door ajar, through which a lady entered unannounced and, at first, unnoticed by me.

Pausing from my duties, I had sat in my favorite armchair, amusing myself by reading Balzac. Engrossed in his *Father Goriot*, I failed to notice the woman until she spoke.

"Sir, do you know where I might find Mr. Carl Brooke?"

She shocked me from my quiet contemplation and I stood a shade too swiftly before smiling, awkwardly correcting for my surprise.

Standing before me was a carefully dressed yet corpulent lady of some fifty years of age. She wore a fragile smile that could not mask an overall seriousness in her demeanor. In contrast to the seriousness, her dress, bright and cheery, seemed more suited for spring than such a muggy summer evening. She rested her right hand firmly upon an exquisitely decorated cane, which had a curiously oversized creamy ivory handle.

With a slight bow and flourish of hands, I said, "Why yes, Madam. He could be found directly in front of you."

Then, quite suddenly, the cane supported a greater weight and any sign of jovial familiarity vanished from her tired face. What now stood before me was a sad figure with a bowed spine and eyes that held a curious mixture of desperation and hope.

She could have been any one of Balzac's Parisian characters of a certain age and disposition. "That elderly young lady," as Balzac had labeled Mlle. Michonneau, would have perfectly described my present visitor. For what I had initially taken for fifty now seemed decades older. What vile and sudden decay her unresolved sadness had caused!

She had, I could immediately recognize, once been a remarkably attractive woman, although wrinkles and the weight of some ugly burden had been for some time squeezing much of its appeal from that youthful charm.

Even so, much like pencil markings that cannot truly be erased once the lead has etched the paper, the remnant youthful beauty and ageless confidence could not go entirely unnoticed even by the dullest of eyes.

"Mr. Brooke, my name is Portia Chodary," she said in a voice little more than a whisper. She paused, her eyes roving about the room, increasingly unsure due to some hidden concern.

Eventually, she continued in an even lower voice. "I am in need of your services. In great need."

Any trace of my previous playfulness disappeared at those words. I fumbled for a handkerchief from my jacket which hung behind the chair. Handing it to her, she immediately blotted away the large tears that were beading up and threatening to burst out of those swollen, sorrowful eyes.

"Please, Mrs. Chodary," I said as I moved my chair for her to sit. "Please."

She accepted the offer, almost falling as though her legs and the walking stick could no longer hold her weight. Having regained her composure somewhat, she placed the cane across her lap.

"My husband," she blurted out before a series of sobs took over; they were quickly squelched by the handkerchief. She lowered her hands and began again in a slightly stronger voice. "My husband has been murdered."

2

"Murdered?" I asked in some alarm.

"Yes. Murdered. A week ago tonight."

"Surely this is a matter for the police. Why..."

"The police believe it to be a natural death," she said and buried her eyes into the handkerchief. "A weakening of the heart, they say."

I frowned. I knew a great deal of our local Boston force—all of whom I held in high professional esteem. Was it possible for the dreadful emotional impact of losing her husband to cause the poor woman to imagine things—to concoct a horrible but illusory circumstance—that simply did not happen?

In this scientific age, it is universally understood that cool, disinterested judgment is superior to rash, emotional impulses—the latter often leading to error.

Yes, but even so, I have always held to the old-fashioned belief that our emotions and intuition often reveal truths invisible and unapproachable by the physical senses. I was, and am, convinced that both intellect and emotion are necessary for a holistic understanding of truth.

I nodded, urging her to continue.

"Yes," she said, "I do admit, it did appear to be a natural cause, but I have grown convinced it was murder, Mr. Brooke, murder through a most devilish means. You will undoubtedly think me mad—as I would have myself but a few months ago. However, once the facts were laid bare, I came to believe the curse was real."

"The curse, madam?"

She nodded. "You see, we have a small pawnbroker's business, Portia's Treasures. The name was my dear husband's desire to honor me. Over the years, we supplemented our inventory with unique oddities from around the world. As our business grew, William, my husband, spent more time traveling in search of interesting stock. Last month, William purchased a large cache of textiles and other materials from a regular wholesaler of ours in Clarkesville. After this transaction, he was approached by another merchant, a man he had never met before. In addition to other items, this merchant sold William a particular ruby. It was, Mr. Brooke, indeed most beautiful."

Mrs. Chodary massaged the cane in her lap as she grappled for her next words.

"I told him to take it to Mr. Baker who buys such things, but William refused. I told him we had never traded in things of such high value and it was not an item that would suit our shop. Even so, he would not part from it." She looked up at me, eyes wide. "The ruby had taken ahold of him, sir. It changed him."

She shifted in her seat and used the handkerchief to pat her moist forehead. The breezeless windows and opened door through which muggy air had seeped only seemed to add to the discomfort.

"There was something very wrong about the ruby and how my William held it in so high regard. Yes, it was beautiful and surely of great value, but something was wrong. I pleaded with him to get rid of the thing. Being of Indian origin..."

"Indian origin, madam?" I asked with some interest.

As a younger man, I had spent a few years in the Indian subcontinent and had been utterly fascinated by certain gemstones from that area. The Romans often spoke of the East, and India in particular, as the progenitor of wealth—the birthplace of prosperity. To the Romans, India held vast caches of emeralds, diamonds, rubies, sapphires—not to mention textiles, fruits, spices, and other items of great wonder—things unheard of in the ancient Western World.

"Yes, that is what the dealer told him when he purchased it. Being of Indian origin, it was not something I expected our clientele to be much interested in purchasing. When William told me the ruby was said to be cursed, I was all the more insistent. He laughed it off as though it were merely an idle tale contrived to elicit a buying interest from customers, but as the days and weeks wore on, he became serious, very gravely serious."

"You say, the ruby changed your husband's demeanor. In what way exactly?"

"Well," she said, shifting in her seat and once again, rubbing the handle of the cane. "We've always been close, my dear William and I, but from the day he purchased that ruby, he started acting terribly aloof, keeping things from me—small things such as the books he was reading or minor purchases for the store. Until that point, he had always been open and honest. Not only that, but he began going off most every night without telling me where. When he returned, as he always did a little over an hour after leaving, he ranted on incoherently about Indian gods, legends, and supernatural stories of previous owners of that cursed ruby."

"Stories?"

She nodded. Eyes wide, she leaned in my direction, her

posture weakening ever so slightly. "Yes, Mr. and Mrs. such-and-such were found dead in their apartment shortly after purchasing the ruby, he'd say, while rubbing the gem incessantly. Another man fell to his death after believing the ruby could make him fly like a bird. Shortly thereafter, to my great horror, my William even said *he* could fly! The absurdity of his statements grew progressively worse. Until... until..."

The tears returned, but underneath the tears were eyes of determination. She placed her cane on the floor and straightened her back.

"Late last Tuesday, I returned from a delivery run to a customer. Upon opening the door, I saw the prone body of my poor dear William. I ran to his side. He was pale—pale as the Angel of Death himself. His eyes were glazed over, but quite suddenly, those eyes turned sharp and looked squarely at mine and then he spoke. In his last breath he said to me, 'The Mad Sheik is not'."

After a few moments of stunned silence, I asked, "Who is this Mad Sheik? And how is he not?"

She seemed unsure of what to say next. "I do not know exactly," she said at last, and quickly added, "but surely it has something to do with the cursed ruby."

"Go on."

"I mentioned my husband began nightly walks?"

"Yes," I said, encouragingly.

"He would disappear for an hour and return a changed man. The night—last Tuesday—after he spoke..."

She paused as a series of sobs prevented words from escaping her throat, her back once again bowed.

"It is all right, dear lady. Would you care to discuss this in the morning? I do have time tomorrow—"

"I'm sorry. I must say this and I must say this now." She cleared her throat, straightened her posture once again, and continued. "After he spoke his final words, I noticed his left hand tightly gripping something as though it were the greatest treasure on earth. Unwrapping his fingers, I backed away in horror."

"The ruby?"

She nodded.

I turned away to collect my thoughts, walking toward the open window and taking in the surprisingly cool evening air. A healing breeze had suddenly appeared—the first of the evening. The familiar clip-clop of a horse buggy filtered up from the street below, the meeting hall being on the second floor. I took a deep breath, clearing my senses. The ambient noises, far from distracting, always seemed to pull my thoughts inward, reordering and organizing them into a focused concentration.

I must admit to having had a fascination with precious stones and the fantastical stories behind them. It had always held a certain romanticism to my heart.

Returning from my silent reverie, I faced Mrs. Chodary. "These nightly walks and his altered personality, you believe your husband's changes had everything to do with the ruby?"

"Yes. He would take the ruby with him each night and each night return with it. After a week of him leaving as my husband and returning as a different person, I followed him one night." She adjusted her weight in her chair and it squeaked in protest. "Well, it wasn't just that. I must admit to having had a secondary concern and reason to follow. While asleep or in a feverous fit, he had on more than one occasion, muttered phrases like 'I need her' or 'where is she?'"

Mrs. Chodary lowered her eyes as if in embarrassment.

"And so, I followed him. I was horrified to find him enter a hotel—the Omni House on Tremont Street. I followed him inside and was only partially set at ease to discover his companion was not a woman, but an aged Arab in traditional dress."

"The Mad Sheik, perhaps?"

She looked back at me and nodded. "I believe him to be the same individual."

"What were they doing, Madam?"

"Talking and drinking tea."

"Tea?"

"Yes, and come to think of it, this was also something that changed in my husband. He drank nothing but tea the last month of his life. Not the regular sort of tea one might buy at the market, mind you. This infusion was more fragrant, and it had to be carefully prepared in a special manner of which he refused to disclose or share. I can only imagine he received the tea from his strange acquaintance at the Omni."

I made a mental note of the two themes: the apparently cursed ruby and the man's tea obsession. And, of course, the possible connection between the two: the Mad Sheik.

3

"Did you overhear the conversation at the hotel?" I asked Mrs. Chodary and held out a platter of biscuits for her refreshment.

She waved a gentle hand refusing the offer.

"I'm afraid not. My husband and I have always had an honest relationship and I only followed him out of a deepest concern. I dared not risk him thinking me anything less than the faithful wife I had always been—especially after I realized he was just meeting someone about one of his fancies."

"'A wife of noble character is worth more than rubies,' saith Solomon the Wise. What were his fancies, as you say?"

"Well, William was very fond of legends and folktales of all sorts. He was particularly interested in anything related to the fantastical or supernatural. It was a hobby...no, more of a passion. He kept a journal of the most interesting myths, legends, and hearsay, and he would pepper any customer or traveler with questions. He believed those fancies, too," she quickly added. "At least he believed certain aspects of all tales to be true. 'No one believes a complete lie, Portia', he would tell me. 'Even the most fantastical lies have some element of truth at their core.'"

I nodded. "This gemstone, did it have a popular name ascribed to it? Do you know anything of its origins?"

"Honestly, sir, I know nothing more about it. It could be priceless and world-renowned, or a piece of glass worthy of the refuse pile. All I know is it was clearly set apart from the second-hand jewelry we normally bought. In the beginning, I thought my husband had been duped into buying a worthless trinket considering the low price he paid for the lot, but now..." she said sobbing softly. "It was such a dreadful thing. And a dreadful thing came out of it. I wish the whole thing were naught but dust blown away in the wind."

"And where is the dreadful thing now?"

She sat silent for a few moments; it seemed as if she was considering her next actions. She then turned her cane upright and unscrewed the top, the oversized creamy ivory handle that I had observed earlier. The handle was soon removed and, tilting the cane, an object wrapped in a white linen handkerchief dropped from the hollow shaft and into her hand. Thrusting the small bundle in my direction, she said, "If this case is of interest to you, I wish this to be the payment."

I took the object and unraveled the cloth. In my hand I held a most exquisite gem. Small, yes, but magnificent. It was multi-faceted with a deep blood-red color. Flawless, absolutely flawless! Using my fingers to pinch the ruby in the cloth, I watched as sparks of life danced within the gem in front of the flickering light emanating from the lamp on my desk.

I realized one thing immediately. The ruby had not come from India. By its peculiar hue, it seemed to me to be of Burmese origin, but I would not say as such to Mrs. Chodary without first consulting an expert. If I were correct, the purchase of the ruby, which had some apparent part in the demise of her husband, had been based on a lie. Since a lie is told for the benefit of some hidden purpose, there was, perhaps, something more to the story. At that precise moment, I determined to help the lady in any way possible.

"It is marvelous," I said, taking in its deep blood-red hue one last time. Carefully wrapping the gemstone, I said, "But I cannot accept such an item. This belongs in a museum, Madam."

"I do not want that thing anywhere near me," she said as she finished returning her handle to the shaft of her cane. "Nor do I want it given to a museum in my name. Take it and do with it as you please, but I will not take the cursed thing back."

At that time, members of the *Agora Society* were not yet in the habit of accepting remuneration for our services and I again refused.

"You will be doing me a great service worth far more than this ruby," she said with a stubborn finality. "If you say you will not receive it, I shall leave here and throw it into the nearest body of water. I do not want that dreadful thing."

"Very well, Mrs. Chodary," I said nodding with a solemn acceptance. "Tell me, on the night of your husband's death, was anything stolen?"

"No." Her face crumpled in confusion. "That's the queer thing. Nothing was stolen, including the one object that may have had the greatest value even though it was in William's hand."

With no obvious monetary motive, I thought it best to review the police file before proceeding.

She bade me visit Sergeant Wicks, the officer who had first arrived after her husband's death. Not only did he have more information regarding the details of her concerns, but he retained, as evidence, items which had been on William Chodary's person.

"Yes, Madam. I will pay the officer a visit in the morning. I would advise you to be prepared should we discover it was simply a natural tragedy. Your husband was at an age where a sudden death would not seem unnatural. The fact that nothing was stolen only fortifies this conclusion." I paused, watching her heart sink. "However, seeing the ruby has stirred my interest in the matter, I would very much like to investigate this further."

"Thank you, sir. You do not know how those words please this old woman's heart."

I held up my hand. "However, I request two objects. The first, the journal your husband kept in which he recorded his fancies."

"I have it at the store. It is yours. And the other?" she said sounding somewhat hopeful.

"If you insist on not keeping the ruby, I insist on finding a proper home for it."

🦋 4 🦋

The next morning, as promised, I visited Sergeant Wicks at the Boston Police Department. Entering the building, I first called on my friend, Captain Barnwell.

As I had hinted to Mrs. Chodary, I believed Sergeant Wicks' conclusion to be quite plausible. Still, having been intrigued by her story, I accepted the ruby, and in doing so, was determined to go beyond first impressions. What was it about the ruby that so adversely affected William Chodary's behavior and personality?

"I'm afraid, this time, the whole affair may not be very interesting," Captain Barnwell said after hearing my questions. He fingered the curved end of his overgrown mustache, as was his way when deep in thought. "I have not closely reviewed the facts of the case, but Wicks is absolutely certain the death was from natural causes."

Captain Barnwell stood and stretched, the bones in his neck crackled as he tilted his head back. "But..." he said through a long sigh, "I know you, Mr. Brooke. You have a remarkable form of stubbornness, the kind that would make mules work themselves into a jealous rage."

Allowing for a rare smile, he grabbed his jacket and motioned toward the doorway.

"Let's review the clues together. But," he said stopping me with his hand, "I must ask you to accept the conclusion wherever the facts lead."

Naturally, I agreed and followed my friend along the hall —our footsteps echoing on the painted brickwork—and into a large room filled with police officers waiting to greet me. I took a considerable pleasure to meet fine young men who had done much to clean up the city. The Boston Police Department had, at that time, only been in existence for a few years. Under the capable direction of Captain Scott F. Barnwell and his men, crime across the city had been greatly reduced.

We approached Sergeant Wicks' desk, to be met with an audible sigh. It was possible that Mrs. Chodary had been as persistent with the Sergeant as she had been with me.

"Mrs. Chodary believes her husband was murdered and the murderer broke into the store to commit the crime," said Sergeant Wicks, crossing his arms and shaking his bald head. "But what possible motive would cause the killer to do such a thing? Nothing was missing and the cause of death appears to be natural. Furthermore, being after hours, the doors to the shop, both front and back, were securely closed and locked."

"What of the man's dying words? 'The Mad Sheik is not...'" I asked.

Sergeant Wicks shook his head once more.

"You weren't there when I first interviewed Mrs. Chodary. She was in a state of pure shock, that lady. Understandable, of course, but quite hysterical and beyond reason—I daresay somewhat near to madness. I have no idea what Mr. Chodary whispered, if anything at all, but whatever it was, I have no doubt it was something other than the nonsensical phrase,

'The Mad Sheik is not'. I believe it was nothing less than the projection of her own imagination."

I nodded. It was indeed a peculiar set of last words. A dying man's faint words heard by the ears of a frantic wife are ripe for misinterpretation. However, she had mentioned her husband's meetings.

"The man her husband met with each night was dressed in Arab attire."

"And there you have it," the Sergeant said, flinging his arms wide for effect. "The wife saw that undoubtedly unusual and memorable scene and thus the incoherent whisperings of a dying man took form in 'the Mad Sheik is not,' within her highly susceptible mind."

"She says her husband had been acting strangely during the weeks leading up to his death."

"He seems to have been a strange one, that Mr. Chodary. Interested in the occult and all that. A little crazy, if you ask me." Sergeant Wicks tapped an index finger to his temple.

"And on Mr. Chodary's person, what articles were discovered?"

"Further proof this was no robbery or murder," Sergeant Wicks said as he reached under his desk and pulled out a bag. Casually dumping the contents on the table, he continued. "I'm sure you know he was holding the ruby. Furthermore, he wore this gold chain connected to a similarly gold timepiece of exquisite detail. Surely, that item, alone, would entice some lower fellow to attempt the burglary," he said, pointing to a truly beautiful watch. "His pockets were empty save for a pocketbook containing eleven dollars, and this small tin of tea leaves. Mrs. Chodary kept the pocketbook; I was about to return these other items."

"Curious," I said.

"Curious, sir?"

"It is no matter," I said, waving my hands dismissively.

"The ruby seems to have been at the heart of things. Were you able to find the wholesaler from whom the man purchased it?"

Another sigh.

"Mr. Brooke, I have already listed all the reasons why this was a natural death. Nothing was stolen. The man was in poor health and at sixty years of age, to have one's heart give out is the least suspicious way to go. As for your mysterious sheik, Boston has become something of an international city in recent years. It would certainly not seem out of place for a man of Mr. Chodary's interests to keep company with strange foreigners. There simply was no reason for us to go to the trouble and public expense for an out-of-town trip."

This was all true and utterly reasonable.

All relevant facts seemed to point to a natural cause of death. The man's age, the locked doors, the absence of theft or motive... However, two relevant and important facts had yet to be established: the origin of the ruby, and Mr. Chodary's odd behavior during his final days.

"Would you mind if I kept the tea?" I asked, framing the question within a smile. "I can deliver it to her once examined."

Sergeant Wicks looked at Captain Barnwell who nodded in approval. "I am wrapping up my notes now. I see no immediate need for it."

I nodded in appreciation and left with the tin in hand with the captain following.

Outside the captain's office, I stopped to open the tin can. Immediately, a fragrant mixture of jasmine and earthy tea leaves flowed forth. It was not a common mixture, but it was tea.

"You know," said my tall friend once we were alone, "when someone says 'curious,' it is customary to explain what the matter of curiosity is. Especially," he said with a broad smile that made the waxed tips of his mustache wiggle, "especially so when that someone is you."

"Apologies, my friend. A wild thought came to mind. A wild, and quite possibly errant thought. Allow me to test my theory just a touch, lest I embarrass myself with a hasty and erroneous explanation."

"Very well. Where do we go next?"

"We? Well, now. Are you joining my little circus?"

"I have some expendable time and thought it might be therapeutic for a recent ailment that has afflicted me sorely."

"And what is this recent ailment?"

"Boredom, sir," he said, his bushy gray eyebrows furrowed and a seemingly authentic sadness flittered within his otherwise gleaming eyes. "Boredom due to my being a manager of adventurers. I sit here all day and pine for excitement. It has been a while since I've chased you chasing some fiend."

"I could rather do for something other than excitement," I said, shuddering with the thought of recent events.

5

The following day, I met the captain outside the entrance of Portia's Treasures, Mrs. Chodary's establishment. He had been examining the objects displayed in the window with obvious interest. As I remember, a certain bowler hat caught his eye; I later bought it as a gift once we had resolved the matter of the Mad Sheik.

We entered the store, but behind the counter was not the expected Mrs. Chodary. Instead, we were greeted by a young man who was busily wrapping a vase for a customer, not currently present.

This young man appeared to be in his early twenties, well groomed, and of exceptionally good cheer. Most noticeably, to my eyes, he had the poise of one with vast worldly experience, which so rarely blends well with youthful energies.

"Welcome," he said. "How may I of be assistance today?" He made a slight bow while folding the last corner of the paper around the vase and setting it aside.

"Good day. Is Mrs. Chodary available?" I asked.

"I am very sorry. She had to meet a client. She will be back shortly."

"Are you an employee, sir?"

Rubbing his hands together as if to remove dirt or grime, the young man sidled around the counter and approached us.

"I am her nephew."

His outstretched hand greeted ours in turn with a firm handshake.

"Mennell Chodary, at your service, gentlemen." The soft smile, however, quickly turned into a sharp frown. "You see, my dear uncle recently passed away. I am here to help my aunt during this difficult time."

"A good and conscientious young man," said the captain with the least amount of expression humanly possible.

Captain Barnwell, when on duty or questioning a suspect, possessed the most remarkable ability to mask all surprise, emotion, and pending questions behind an unreadable facade. His bushy gray mustache hid the top lip, masking the fleeting and slight reactions that are so hard to conceal on a clean-shaven face. Through our many years of friendship, I had seen him unnerve the steadiest criminal simply through the way in which he spoke—or more often through the way he remained silent. Unfortunately, he could be equally intimidating to the innocent.

"Thank you, but enough of this sad talk. How may I be of assistance, sirs? After all, the store must sell something or else my poor aunt will have all the more to worry about." The nephew smiled broadly. "I noticed your interest in the bowler hat. This particular example is of exquisite..."

"Actually," I said, "we are here on account of your uncle's passing."

The nephew frowned and stepped back a pace. "I thought the police concluded their investigation."

"Yes, indeed. I am here at the behest of your aunt. My name is Carl Brooke, and this is Captain Barnwell of the

Boston Police. It seems she believes your uncle's death to have been deliberate."

The young man hesitated before asking, "Do you mean murder, sir?"

"Yes."

The young man sighed. "I didn't want to mention this, but my aunt's emotional state isn't the most stable at the moment." The young man crossed his arms and looked down. He spoke slowly and with apparent concern. "She has been through so much, and I believe the extreme emotional experience of recent days has hampered her ability to reason." He looked back up at us and continued. "Quite understandable, really. Even now, she still has the occasional hysterical fit and has taken to the belief some silly curse was the cause of her misfortunes."

The youth's words echoed those of Sergeant Wicks, true. However, the woman who had appeared before me the previous evening had shown none of that. Emotional, yes, but in no way hysterical.

"For her sake, I do hope it was not murder," I said with a polite smile. "It would be a terrible thing for her husband to have had his life shortened unnaturally," I paused for a cough, an old habit of mine, as a way to insert a pause when gauging reactions. The captain had his mustache; I had my cough. I've found even most innocent people hide information whether out of guilt, fear, or even ignorance of it themselves. In the nephew, I saw not the hint of dishonesty, only genuine concern.

"I must admit a more selfish interest," I said continuing. "I am most interested in the ruby that seems to have had some significance to your uncle during his final days. Do you have access to her records? I would like to know from whom the ruby was purchased."

The nephew looked at the captain. "You are police, sir?"

"I am," Captain Barnwell said, extracting his credentials and flashing them to before the young man. "We would be much obliged if you'd look that up for us."

"Well, I suppose if Aunt Portia wishes it... Give me a moment while I search the records."

While the nephew disappeared to a back room, we examined the store.

It held a magnificent and encyclopedic collection of antiques, trinkets, and objects of casual decoration many of which appeared to be more than one hundred years old. As Mrs. Chodary had said, however, the items, while interesting, were not on the scale of the ruby.

My eyes fell upon a bonnet the likes of which my grandmother would have thought fashionable in her youth. Next to the bonnet, a stack of postage stamps carried the likeness of a European monarch I could not immediately place.

Turning toward the store entrance, a striking statue of three monkeys stared directly at me. It was large, about a foot high and twice that wide. The monkeys sat upon a pedestal adjacent to the door—the first object any visitor would notice. One monkey covered its eyes, another covered its ears, and the last covered its mouth. I had seen that motif often while traveling the Orient.

Protruding from the base was a cranked metal bar which I took to be a winding mechanism. Was it a music box?

"It is a most ugly thing," said the young man, noticing the object in my view. He returned to us carrying a box. "Those monkeys always seem to be looking directly at me as if to accuse me of some heinous crime. Well, at least two of them."

I nodded. To my eyes, it was well-crafted, although not a piece I would keep on display. It was obviously of some age. A few patches of dark brown felt had fallen off the see-no-evil monkey's face and a few tears spoiled the clothing the creatures wore.

"Anyway, I've searched the receipt box, but I cannot find such a record. It would have been in the last two months, surely, but there are no Clarkesville receipts. Furthermore, I am certain there are no receipts recording the large amount he would have spent in acquiring the ruby."

The young man placed the box on the counter for our examination. Indeed, a receipt for such a large purchase should be easy to find in a box so neatly organized. There were a handful of invoices from the previous month, but all were from local wholesalers and for purchases of goods worth less than fifty dollars.

"As I stated," said the youth, "I think the emotional state of my..."

A ringing bell greeted us as the door opened and in stepped Mrs. Chodary, using her walking cane to shut the door behind her.

"Ah, Mr. Brooke, Captain, thank you so much for coming."

Far from hysterical, the lady once again appeared to be as calm and completely in her right mind as she had been the night before.

"A most interesting collection of items you have here, Mrs. Chodary," I said, walking over to greet her.

"It was my husband's idea. His passion, actually. 'Items guaranteed to catch your eye, not your pocketbook,' as he would often say. We spent decades building this business." A flash of sadness covered her face, but only a flash. She looked up smiling and said, "So, how can I help you help me?"

"Now, Auntie," said the youth, "don't get all worked up about this. It was simply Uncle William's time. Why don't you just sit..."

"Don't patronize me!"

She spoke with a ferocity quite unlike her previously lady-like demeanor.

"I apologize," she said to us. "My nephew is trying to comfort me, but," turning to him, she said, "Mennell, you must understand. I watched my husband, your uncle, deteriorate rapidly and unnaturally. I saw him meet with strange people and act in an equally strange way. I heard my husband's dying words—mock them as you may. I held him as he died. There is something much more to this, and I mean to find out what that something is."

Her speech was passionate, but hardly hysterical. There was emotion, but emotion backed by reason; indeed, emotion properly placed can make reason all the more rational and human.

"There does seem to be something worthy of investigation," said the captain. "If anything, I'd like to know whether the purchase of the ruby is in any way connected with your husband's nightly escapades."

"Indeed," I said. "Let's start out with the purchase—the one with the ruby. Do you know the wholesaler's name and address?"

"I'm afraid not. My husband met the person somewhere in Clarkesville while I stayed behind minding the store." She touched her chin with her index finger and said, "Come to think of it, the whole thing was rather unexpected. After leaving a long-time customer—the purpose for his trip, the dealer in question, a stranger, approached him on the street. I'm afraid that's all I know about what actually happened, but we should have the contact information in the receipt box."

"Unfortunately, your nephew was unable to produce the receipt."

"Well, it should be here," she said. Noticing the box the nephew had brought out, she thumbed through the bills of purchases. After a few seconds, she said, "Very strange." She raised one eyebrow in a questioning slant and pursed her lips.

"It was here. I know. I put it here myself," she said, tapping her finger on the side of the box a few times. "But no matter."

Mrs. Chodary sauntered uneasily around the counter and leaning down, reappeared moments later with an oversized ledger book. "Thankfully, my husband was rather fastidious with such matters." Turning the large pages, she examined the book and landed a heavy finger on the last marked page. "Here," she said with some excitement. "Oh, my. Aladdin's Lamp." She looked directly at me. "That's the name of the merchant's store. The Sheik... It appears the Mad Sheik followed my poor husband here and killed him."

"Let's not jump ahead of the facts, Ma'am," Captain Barnwell said, straightening to his imposing full height—every bit the commanding police officer.

"I do apologize. I was just...I didn't imagine there could have been a connection between the dealer in Clarkesville and the man my husband met each night."

"A most curious yet possible connection, Mrs. Chodary, to be sure. Does the receipt record the Sheik's name or address?"

"I have his calling card here attached to the ledger. It simply reads, 'the Sheik'," she said, handing me a rectangular shaped card with the Sheik's contact information. "His address is in Clarkesville."

I received the card with a slight bow. "Thank you, Mrs. Chodary. I'll ask for your husband's commonplace book and we will be on our way for today."

"Oh, yes, of course. Just a moment." As she crouched below the counter in search of the diary, I stole a quick glance at the nephew. He did not seem at all happy. His arms were crossed tightly, matching equally tight lips. There did seem to be a strained tension between the aunt and nephew. Perhaps he felt he was doing what was best for her or perhaps he had his own agenda. Either way, it was apparent she did not appreciate his concern.

She reappeared a moment later with a tattered book and extended it toward me. I took the book and examined its initial pages, realizing its importance immediately.

The man had spent many hours in careful study and even more time recording his thoughts of importance. His handwriting was large but magnificent, betraying a man whose eyesight had weakened, but not his mind. Smaller notes in the margins showed a man who often reviewed his earlier thoughts and reassessed old beliefs and knowledge. It was a commonplace book—one into which a man may pour his soul: poems, verses, thoughts, and quotes. I nodded at her, knowing what a treasure she had bestowed.

"His eyesight became weaker this past year, I'm afraid. You can see how large his letters had become."

I nodded, closing the book and placing it in my inner coat pocket.

"We shall examine this closely and return it to you safely upon concluding our investigation. Thank you, Mrs. Chodary," I said with a slight bow to the lady and then to her nephew. At first glance, a hint of coldness sharpened his steely eyes, but an instant later, the coldness was gone and the nephew's demeanor quickly reverted to the jovial sort of fellow he was when first we arrived. The change was so quick, so complete, it almost had me disbelieving what I saw.

"It was so nice to have met you," said the nephew now with warm and happy eyes. "I do hope we can meet again soon."

❧ 6 ❧

"W hat is your opinion of the young man, Captain?" I asked as we walked away from the store.

He placed his large hand on my shoulder stopping both of us.

"It may well be he has his aunt's best interests in mind, but he and his aunt seem to be on opposing sides as to what those interests may be."

I nodded.

"I can't imagine," he continued, "that the lad had any hand in his uncle's strange behavior and ultimate death, but..." His voice dropped to a whisper, "but I would not be surprised if his present kindness to his aunt has some monetary purpose behind it."

"Yes, it would seem there is something more to young Mennell's desire to help," I said.

"I am afraid I will have little time the rest of today and much of tomorrow, but might I suggest attempting to confirm Mrs. Chodary's story? She claimed Mr. Chodary acted strangely the days before his death. The nephew hinted that was one of his aunt's hysterics, which places one of the two at odds with easily verifiable facts."

"Yes, one or the other isn't telling us the whole story." I nodded. "I will report to you my findings."

Captain Barnwell and I parted ways with a handshake and a mutual understanding of the circumstances. He returned to his precinct, while I attended to a long-forgotten work-related chore at my bank.

Upon the completion of that chore, I had thought to go to my house for lunch and study William Chodary's diary. I wanted to know if it held answers to Captain Barnwell's question, or if Wicks and the nephew were correct regarding their view of Mrs. Chodary's instability. My experiences with her were directly the opposite.

Did Mr. Chodary's health deteriorate in an unnatural way as the aunt said, or would his last entries show a mind sharp to the end? Was there any mention of meeting the Sheik, or was that also a product of her imagination? And if there was a Sheik, what was his relationship to the dead man?

I patted my side pocket, the pocket holding that precious book, resisting the urge to pull it out while walking along the street.

As I rounded the corner of Third and Bartley, a peculiar feeling overtook me, and I had to stop.

As I have mentioned in previous letters, there have been moments in my life during which I have experienced inexplicable extra-sensory knowledge. It is as if I am able to gain knowledge from some unquantifiable sense beyond taste, sight, touch, smell, and hearing. Perhaps my entire past experience is somehow used unconsciously to filter and categorize all the information around me.

Whatever the reason, my suspicions were aroused, and I had the uncanny feeling of being watched.

I slowly, and casually stooped down as if to pick a penny

from the ground. As I did so, I pulled a small mirror from my ticket pocket, and held it as if that was the object I had found on the ground.

I used this brief moment to survey the scene behind me. There were a few people walking down the block, but no one appeared suspicious in the slightest. No one, except a lone figure, smoking a cigarette; he was turned away from me in the distance. I was quite certain the man had been the source of my peculiar sensation.

Pocketing the mirror, I stood and brushed off my pant legs. Immediately, I picked up my pace, turned the first corner, and, with the spirit of a much younger man, ran full speed and turned the next two corners. My agility was rewarded with what my intuition had only hinted.

"Ah, Mr. Mennell Chodary. Fancy seeing you here."

The youth clearly was not expecting my presence, especially from behind him. He had begun walking toward my previous location. Having flicked his half-smoked cigarette onto the cobblestone, the young man was increasing his speed when I engaged him with my question.

His lips twitched; he had the same cold, steely eyes I had seen earlier, a set of hollow eyes that seemed haunted by an inner torment.

An instant later, the surprise and coldness disappeared. The hollow eyes were now dancing, and the cold eyes had turned warm with hospitality. It was a most remarkable turnaround. If I hadn't experienced the act twice, I would be, once again, hard-pressed to believe it.

"Yes, Mr. Brooke. It is a small world, isn't it?"

"Indeed. A small world makes it easy for one to follow another. You might tell me why you were following me?"

"Ah, I apologize."

He looked down to his well-polished shoes—expensive material, expertly crafted, and immaculately maintained. In his waistcoat pocket was a gold pocket watch with a hunter-case. It appeared to be of Swiss design—also expensive.

"Yes, Mr. Brooke, I was following you. I wanted to tell you something, but I wasn't sure if I should. Unfortunately, that hesitation made me appear rather ill-mannered."

"You might as well tell me now."

"Yes, sir. Please, sir, for her sake, halt your investigation."

"You do understand, I am investigating at your aunt's request."

"You see, sir, I didn't want to say it, especially not in front of her, but I believe my aunt is suffering from some form of dementia. She forgets things—not regularly, but when she does it's obvious. Not only that, but she sometimes speaks of things which never happened. I fear her imagination has overtaken her. I think this business with the so-called Mad Sheik is one such example. Please, I beg you, hand over my uncle's diary and let this matter rest. My poor aunt needs comfort, not a rehashing of the horrible events of recent days."

I looked the man over, his hand extended hoping to receive the diary. Indeed, he did seem to be genuinely concerned for his aunt's well-being, but, I remembered those previously hollow and cold eyes.

"My uncle wasn't in the best of condition," said the nephew, continuing, "and as you said earlier, leading her to believe it was anything other than a natural death would be cruel."

Of course, at face value, the youth's words made sense. Moreover, Sergeant Wick's words mirrored his. Could this be much ado about nothing? Could I be causing undue harm by playing into the sentimentality of a grieving woman?

I could only attest to what I had seen.

Considering her state of mind in my presence, both at the club and at her shop, I could see her only as wholly coherent with a rational disposition. I could hardly call her recounting of the tragedy as mad ravings.

Besides, questions were building in my own mind. What connection did the Arab have with the ruby? Her husband's newly found love of Oriental tea—could Mrs. Chodary simply have imagined those factual details when she was otherwise without control of her faculties? These questions could be easily verified by Mr. Chodary's commonplace book and a few well-placed questions among his acquaintances. Furthermore, a visit to the hotel in question may give me the answers I required.

"Thank you. I will certainly take that under advisement, but you must understand who I am, sir." I leaned into his space, watching closely for any change in his expression or movement of aggression. "If there is a murderer on the loose, however small the chance, I must, by honor of being a gentleman, discover the truth."

There it was again. A moment, a flash, something indescribable and so quickly discarded that one would feel obliged to disbelieve one's own eyes had it not become inescapable by multiple repetitions in my presence. A shadow had blanketed the youth's now clear eyes. Momentarily, yes, and just as momentarily, it was gone.

"I will briefly examine this book, and once done, it will be returned to your aunt."

Smiling, the youth withdrew his hand and said, "Certainly sir. I understand one must not go against one's sense of honor. I only ask that once you are satisfied all of this is in the realm of imagination, you will make it as plain as you can to my aunt. Tell her my uncle died peacefully and naturally. Tell her there is no silly curse or a devilish Arab. It will do her some measure of good to hear it from you. Of that, I am certain."

With a good day, I turned, determined to gather more

information before returning home. After my little detour with Mennell, I was but a block away from the hotel Mr. Chodary had allegedly met with the Sheik.

Perhaps I could determine how much of Mrs. Chodary's story was based on reality. Perhaps I could finally discover the liar.

7

Built in 1835, the five-story stone and brick building gleamed with a beautiful white marble facing. It had a lavish and welcoming charm and—it struck my senses with its magnificence—a curious mixture of the untouchable sublime and a mother's warm embrace.

Entering the lobby of the Omni House, I delighted in the grand interior architecture. I could imagine spending many a carefree hour admiring the marble foyer and the large lobby with its arched windows set in richly finished walls.

A hint of scented flowers and spices from some hidden potpourri sent my thoughts to faraway India. A fitting setting for a leisurely conversation with the "Mad Sheik."

To my right, a number of chairs sat upon a large, thick rug. Perhaps this was the area used for their nightly meetings.

I turned to my left and proceeded to the reception desk. It was time to determine if Mrs. Chodary's mind had given into fantasy completely—or if there were other facets of this matter to be discovered.

"Good day," I said to the receptionist, a young man wearing a bright red uniform. "Could you tell me if you've seen in the recent past an Arab gentleman taking nightly tea frequently with another gentleman?"

"Oh, the Sheik. Not recently. Are you a friend of the man, sir?"

Shaking my head in the negative, I asked, "You say he's called the Sheik?"

The young man leaned in close to me.

"He referred to himself as the Sheik of some foreign land or another and made himself out to be someone of importance, but he hasn't been in the hotel for over a week. At least, I haven't seen or heard anything of him in the last few days. He became quite the topic of conversation among the staff with his peculiar dress and speech. Prior to this week, I saw the Sheik and your friend for over a month on a regular basis. Almost like clockwork and every night. Truth be told, I've been worried. I noticed your friend leaving, often looking as if he was ill. I suppose he still hasn't shaken whatever it is."

"No, he has not. I am here on behest of his wife. She wishes me to find the Sheik in order that I may issue him an invitation to meet tonight with her husband in their home. In addition, my friend has tasked me to locate his pocket watch key which he fears he left near his chair when he last met the Sheik." I straightened my back, looked around, and, returning my gaze to the young man's eyes, asked, "Would you mind pointing out which chair he occupied?"

The receptionist frowned and arched a finger to the corner of the seating area I had noticed earlier.

"They were always in the corner with the table, chair, and bench. The Sheik always sat on the bench with his back to the lobby. The other man occupied the chair, but I am quite certain the watch key has not been found. We keep the lobby in order, cleaning every night."

"As a matter of curiosity, what did they do during their meetings?"

The receptionist shrugged. "They would sit for a half hour every night drinking tea and engaging in a very one-sided conversation. Every night. The Sheik would order a pot of hot water and brew the tea. While the other man enjoyed the tea, the Sheik lectured. Your friend rarely spoke but took copious notes in a small notebook."

My hand reached into my coat pocket and retrieved Mr. Chodary's commonplace book.

"Was this his book?"

"Yes, that looks very much the same size and color."

Mrs. Chodary's mind had not played tricks on her. She had, indeed, witnessed her husband and the Sheik. It did not rule out, however, the possibility her over-active mind had translated an innocent meeting into murder.

"Would you describe the Sheik in the event I see him on the street?"

"You would immediately recognize him, sir. Arab dress, full head scarf, large white beard. He also wore oversized and tinted spectacles. I never saw him in Western garb. He spoke with a heavy accent and used queer idiomatic expressions."

"I see. Do you happen to know what topics of conversation crossed their lips?"

"I'm afraid not. I am a good distance away, but, of course, I also make it a point to not listen on our guests."

"Naturally. Do you know what sort of tea they enjoyed?"

"What sort, sir?"

"Apologies. I'm wondering if something he ingested—perhaps from this hotel—could have caused my friend's illness."

The man bridled. "Oh, I assure you, all foods and drinks served here are of the highest quality. The tea brewed by the Sheik was brought by the man himself. The hotel supplied the hot water, only."

"I see. The Arab was a patron of this hotel, no?"

"I believe he was, sir."

"You believe? Is there a recourse to ascertain his name? It would be of great benefit for my friend if I could speak with him."

He reached below, retrieved a large ledger, and tapped the closed cover.

"I don't remember seeing any foreign names, nor do I remember his arrival. Of course, I'm not always here at the reception desk. My additional duties take me away at different times."

"Yet, you believe he was a guest?"

"Yes. Every time your friend met the Sheik, he would appear from the hotel stairs and after each evening's tea, he would exit the same way." The receptionist put his hand to his chin and added, "Actually, I never saw him leave the hotel."

"You never saw him leave?" I said, almost absent-mindedly.

"No sir, but as I said, I am not here all day and every day."

"Might I have a look?" I asked pointing to the large book before the receptionist.

The man appeared aghast. "I am afraid not, sir. The Omni House considers its guests personal information to be sacred."

I pulled a few bank notes from my money clip and placed it on the counter in front of him. "I will only inspect the names for, say, sixty seconds."

The receptionist looked around, eyes scanning the empty lobby behind me. He placed the large book on the counter and took the money.

"I'll be back in two minutes," and then promptly disappeared through an office door.

I opened the large book. As I flipped the pages, I saw

many entries from the previous five weeks, but none were outside common European names.

Closing the book, I said in the direction of the closed office door, "Your assistance has been very helpful, my good man."

Thinking of the little book in my pocket, I took my leave.

❧ 8 ❧

I immediately made my way to my home, my head filled with thoughts of the mysterious "Sheik" and what answers the little book may hold.

The fact the Sheik was real and Mrs. Chodary's husband had met with him confirmed her assertions. What did these facts mean in regard to the nephew's behavior? He was, after all, quite convinced the Sheik was merely a symptom of his aunt's failing mental health.

Maneuvering upstairs to my library, I settled into my reading chair, a Morris of some age. I had just learned Mr. Chodary had taken notes during the Sheik's nocturnal lectures. This greatly increased my curiosity and my desire for concentrated reading time.

I pulled out the book, held it up to the light from my window, and admired its tattered form. Mr. Chodary's book was a fine commonplace book. Small and leather-bound, the book bore decorative brass corners, and its appearance showed careful and loving use over many months.

I opened the book and thumbed carefully through the pages. There were approximately two hundred pages, three quarters of which had been filled with over a year's worth of entries.

Early pages held quotes and reading notes, clearly showing the inquisitiveness and sharp mind of an avid reader. Toward the end of the book, the end of his life, however, the entries were decidedly esoteric and, occasionally, meaningless. His handwriting had deteriorated at a quite rapid pace as well—the final two weeks, markedly so.

Yes, his poor eyesight meant his letters were consistently large from the beginning, but were carefully written. The final pages, however, were little more than scribblings. Once again, I had another undeniable fact which supported Mrs. Chodary's account of events. Whatever the cause of Mr. Chodary's ailment and subsequent death, it did not agree with the assumption of a sudden demise.

I turned my attention and concentration to the pages prior to the changes Mrs. Chodary had earlier reported.

One entry contained the first mention of the newly purchased gem, and what followed were several pages spent in description of the ruby. It had clearly captured his imagination. The pages were filled with meditations on the ruby and queer stories about other rare gems, surely learned from the Sheik.

A few pages later, he wrote the following:

"Today marks the beginning of a new kind of understanding. Today, I met the Sheik, Mr. Abdul's business associate. Under his tutelage, I have begun to discover the great mysteries that lie within her."

He had started the curious habit of referring to the ruby as "she" or "her" a week earlier. This was undoubtedly the "her" that Mrs. Chodary had been so worried about; the concern which caused her to follow her husband to the hotel. I immediately understood the reference.

The rest of the page was left blank, but the following page, dated two days later included this peculiar line:

"Last night, she called to me. There are things she can do while guided by the Sheik, things that are unnatural, verily impossible. I can see many ethereal things. I fear I go mad, but while in this madness, I can see many things impossible. So real. Yes. So full of meaning in the moment and yet impossible to fully recall once out of the moment. As the morning arrives, there departs all the pertinent details and meaning. Only the faint memory of some hidden genius remains. That, and of course the madness."

The subsequent pages devolved further into nonsense. Syntax and basic spelling conventions were ignored. The last recorded page simply states, "Fly! Fly! I can fly."

Within three days, the man would be dead.

I CAN FLY.

I let those words play in my mind.

I can see many things impossible.

Something had happened to the man during that time. It had to do with the ruby, the "her." It had to do with the Sheik, his mentor and the business partner of the merchant. But most importantly, it had to do with the tea.

I set the book to the side and opened the tin can I had received from Sergeant Wicks. Hint of Jasmine and black tea. But there was some other exotic fragrance my mind could not place.

The Sheik made appearances and disappearances from within the hotel, but there was not a confirmed record of his stay.

I can see many things impossible. I can fly.

I closed the book, placed it in my inner coat pocket, and made the decision to travel to Clarkesville.

If I could not find the Sheik, I would find the next best thing: the merchant from whom Mr. Chodary had purchased the ruby. One, Mr. Abdul.

❧ 9 ❧

That evening we had a club meeting.

The *Agora Society*, as always, was filled with professionals, scholars, and clergymen; all had a singular desire to affect the betterment of mankind. Our collective professions, expertise, and inquisitiveness made our unofficial investigations possible, and, I daresay inevitable.

Before the meeting officially began, I pulled Dr. Morgan aside. I had need of an answer to a medical question.

I told him what the aunt had said about her husband's last days, and I showed him the relevant passages from the diary, giving special attention to the final entries.

"Do you know of a slow-acting poison that would cause these symptoms and lead to death?"

"Poison?" the doctor asked while flipping the pages of the diary. "From Captain Barnwell's description, it sounded as if the man's heart had simply given out."

"Yes, and that very well may be the case. However, one must be skeptical, to a fault, regarding these conflicting accounts. Do you know of a substance that could cause these symptoms?"

The doctor took a deep breath and said, "By the clear deterioration of both mind and hand," he said after turning to the final written page, "it does appear the ultimate cause of death had something to do with those feverish symptoms. And yes, the symptoms could have been caused by various poisons or, even, natural substances."

"Can you hazard a guess to which?"

"It would be difficult to do so without an examination of the body and, even then, it may be impossible to tell. But, it could be any number of substances: an opiate, arsenic, or even," he said, pausing in thought, "an allergic reaction to a common plant."

"If the substance was mixed into a liquid to be consumed unknowingly..."

"A liquid? It would have to be a substance that would be easily dissolved and lacking a tell-tale odor."

"I am thinking of a substance that could be put into tea and would be, as you said, tasteless and odorless. Something, perhaps, used in the Arabian world. And," I paused, considering the absurdity of my words, "must induce a sensation of flying."

"Flying?" The doctor stifled a fit of laughter, and then became serious. He showed not a trace of his previous mirth.

Giving his chin a somber rub, he said, "I do remember reading of a plant in Arabia the Bedouin use as a way to induce hallucinations. It may also induce the sensation of flight. It is used at certain coming-of-age ceremonies which are designed to herald a spiritual rebirth, as it were. Henbane is the plant. It is not common in our parts of the world, but in Asia, henbane is a weed. It is said to produce symptoms very much like those found in the diary."

"The sensation of flying, you say?"

"Yes, that has been reported."

"Could this be given in tea?"

"Yes, according to local custom, the ancient Bedouins would use tea. It was, specifically, a special fragrant tea made from jasmine flowers."

"Jasmine?" I said, fingering the tin can in my pocket.

"They crushed the dried leaf of henbane into a powder and ingest it with the jasmine tea."

"Would you be able examine this for henbane?"

The doctor accepted the can and opened it.

"I will consult my books on the plant and try to give you a definite answer."

I thanked the doctor and sat through most of the meeting, but my mind was greatly distracted knowing I need to confer with Captain Barnwell. I left the meeting a few minutes early and made my way to his home.

There was no doubt in my mind.

William Chodary was murdered.

🦋 10 🦋

Having discussed my findings with the captain, I visited Mrs. Chodary the following morning.

Once again, she was out, and her nephew was minding the store. I could not help but notice the young man's displeasure at my arrival. I had anticipated his reaction, after our awkward confrontation the previous day, and I carried a gift of appeasement.

"Mr. Chodary," I said. "I was wondering if I might have a few words with you."

"Mr. Brooke, I am very busy at the moment and as soon as my aunt returns, I have to leave that instant on important business."

"I have brought you a gift from my time spent in India," I said, handing him a nondescript brown bag.

"A gift? From India? Whatever for?" The young man asked with obvious surprise.

"I could not help but notice you are a fellow tea connoisseur. Here, take a look," I said, as I motioned with my hands that he should open the bag. "Not entirely dreadful, I hope."

Unfolding the bag's top, a waft of a nostalgic aroma reached my senses. It instantly propelled me to a time when, as a young man, I chased grand adventure the world over.

"I made the acquaintance of a civil surgeon called Arthur Campbell. He had cultivated a distinct type of tea from seeds purloined by Robert Fortune."

"Ah, yes," said the young man. "Robert Fortune, the Scottish botanist who single-handedly broke the Chinese monopoly on tea production. If I have my history correct, Mr. Fortune pretended to be Chinese which allowed him to collect thousands of the highest quality plants and seeds."

"Precisely—and at great risk to his life, I might add. You do know your tea lore," I said with a smile. "Mr. Fortune gave Mr. Campbell his seeds, and thus began high-quality tea production in the Darjeeling area."

"Did you know Mr. Fortune?" the young man asked with apparent genuine interest.

"Well, no. I never had the pleasure, but, Mr. Campbell gave me several of Mr. Fortune's specimens for my own cultivation. This is the fruit from one of those plants."

"Much obliged, sir. It is indeed a marvelous gift."

"Tell me, did you often speak with your uncle about your shared love of tea?"

The young man seemed taken aback by my question.

"My uncle, sir? I'm afraid not. I wasn't aware he was a connoisseur as well. Ah, my aunt returns."

I turned to see her shadow pass the window.

"And, as I mentioned, I must take my leave, I'm afraid," he said, clutching his tea. "Please forgive me for my uncivilized actions yesterday. I do thank you for the tea. I shall enjoy it immensely."

As the door opened, I watched the nephew nod to his aunt and exit the moment after she entered. Moving my eyes from the door to the incoming Mrs. Chodary, I noticed something was missing: the three monkeys, which had been prominently displayed near the entrance.

"A young man with refined tastes is a rarity these days, don't you agree?" I said as Mrs. Chodary placed a bag and her cane on the counter. "He has the air and experience of an older and well-traveled man."

"I only wish knowledge could be traded for wisdom."

"Madam?"

She shook her head and raised a hand.

"Please, do not read too much into my comments; the lad has been through quite a bit in recent years. Barely in his twenties now, he's been on his own since his parents had their terrible accident at sea three years ago."

I frowned. "I can only imagine your husband and yourself must have been a great source of strength for him."

"No." She looked away and slowly shook her head. "Although, it was not from lack of trying. My husband made monthly trips to Clarkesville for a while after the accident. Each time, our nephew was cold and distant. He refused even the slightest affections. So, my William soon stopped making the trips. We wrote regularly after that, but our letters were either ignored or returned unopened." She looked back at me. "You see Mr. Brooke, my husband's brother left our nephew a substantial inheritance. The will stated half of it was to be given to him immediately. The other half was to be held by William and me. He was not to receive the remaining sum until we deemed he had a stable mind and settled occupation."

"But you deemed he had neither?"

"We told him as gently as we could, but he saw us as thieves and would have nothing to do with us. For a while, that initial amount of money was all he needed. We tried to be there for him since we were the only family he had left, but he rejected our every offer." She shook her head once again, but continued more hopefully. "However, since my William's passing, Mennell seems to be have discovered the value of family. He hasn't once brought up his inheritance. Not once."

"Perhaps," I said, "his earlier rough behavior was his way of coping with the loss of his parents."

She nodded weakly and began to walk behind the counter.

"If I may ask," I said, nodding toward the empty space by the door, "did you sell the three monkeys?"

"Oh, goodness no," she said, laughing. "Who would want to buy such a monstrosity? At any rate, it was not for sale." She puckered her lips in thought or perhaps in disgust. "My nephew simply hates the thing and most likely, he has hidden it somewhere. Funny how he hates it so, especially since it was his mother who gifted it to us years ago." She bent down behind the counter and reappeared holding the display saying, "Just as I suspected."

Although large and gaudy in appearance, I admired its exquisitely crafted form. The monkeys appeared to be porcelain and were covered in felt. The process of aging had made the felt uneven, exposing small areas of porcelain underneath. Each monkey was fully clothed with a miniature made-to-order suit. Other than a few small tears, the clothes had not faded and appeared to be clean.

"The Three Mystic Apes," she said, patting one of the monkey's heads, "as they are called, represent the ancient proverb, 'see no evil, hear no evil, speak no evil.' In the West, they have come to represent turning one's eye from evil, that one should allow evil to be evil—a most despicable corruption of the original Oriental meaning of..."

"That one should shun evil. One should avoid speaking, hearing, or seeing that which is evil."

"Precisely." She smiled. "It is indeed a monstrosity—my nephew is right about that, but my William was quite fond of it which is why it remained at the entrance and without a price tag, so all could enjoy it. On occasion, a customer would stop to stare at the eyesore. My husband would see the customer's puzzled look and say, 'Pardon, Madam, but the Three Mystic Apes are not for sale.' Of course, I highly doubt any customer ever had an actual desire to purchase the ugly thing." She smiled, fondly remembering her husband's endearing eccentricities. "Watch this."

She reached for the metal bar, gave it a good crank, and pulled the small lever which released the tension; the hidden cylinder began to spin.

A most melodious tune came forth. A few bars later, she moved the lever back to its place, stopping the sound.

"The song is 'Blood is Thicker than Water'," she said, smiling. "It was Mennell's mother's favorite melody."

"A most interesting piece," I said, wondering why the young man would so dislike an object that had been dear to his mother.

"Well," she said, looking me directly in the eye, "have you come to any conclusion on the matter?"

"The matter, madam?"

"Are you speaking with a woman bereft of her senses or a woman bereft of her husband taken by murder?"

"I take your concerns very seriously, madam," I said, bowing slightly. "If you don't mind my asking, is your nephew in school, or, does he have a profession?"

"He attends a university in Clarkesville. I was worried he was missing classes, but he said family is more important than his classes. He won't have to worry about money for now as he has his first half of the inheritance, but I think an education will be vital for the future. Even with the second half of the inheritance, it won't provide for him his whole life."

"Do you have the name of the university?"

She shook her head. "I asked him, but he only said he took leave with the permission of his professors. But I do know it is in Clarkesville."

Clarkesville. There were only two schools of higher education in Clarkesville at that time. Mount Solace and Middlesex. I had investigated Mrs. Chodary's statements and had proven them true. I knew at that point, I must investigate the assertions made by Mennell. It was vital to find and visit his university in Clarkesville—I needed impressions from others who had been in his company.

I changed the subject matter with Mrs. Chodary by asking, "Please tell me, once more, anything at all specific about your husband's behavior the last few days prior to his passing?"

"Yes. You were correct in putting emphasis on those last days; for those days were a striking departure from his normal self. He had a constant fear of losing the ruby; he always kept it on his person. I tried to engage him in conversation, but when he answered, his speech was slurred. At night, he mumbled incomprehensible words and phrases. He often burned with a fever; why, his face turned red from the heat. I tried to convince him to see a doctor, but he refused."

"Did the fevers abate by morning?"

"At first, he would wake up normally as he did before he bought that accursed ruby. Of the previous night's madness? No recollection at all. I'd implore him to stay with me in the afternoons. Each time he said he needed to meet with the Sheik; that he needed to learn from him."

"He met the old Arab that fateful day, I assume?"

"Yes, every evening and without fail. I begged him not to leave as I saw the nightly fevers grow progressively worse, but he said he must go and it was the only thing that could help him. 'Help him with what,' I asked, but he would simply hang his head and cry."

With that scene in my mind, I thanked Mrs. Chodary for her time and quietly left the store.

❦ II ❧

The next morning, I paid a visit to the captain. I related to him Mrs. Chodary's additional information and the captain agreed it was a matter in need of further investigation.

Mrs. Chodary's story had been confirmed, and it could not be dismissed as senile folly. My attention shifted to the nephew. His adamant attitude from the moment of our first meeting, compounded by his curious behavior at our strange meeting on the street, made him the focus of my inquiry.

It was time for us to visit Clarkesville. What were the circumstances behind the transaction of the ruby? Why did the nephew leave his university?

The captain was eager to join me on my journey to Clarkesville and I agreed. His company would serve as ballast to drive home the seriousness of the matter to those we were to interview.

After reaching Clarkesville, an easy journey in the comfort of the captain's carriage, and armed with Mrs. Chodary's calling card, we made our way to the address of the dealer who had sold the ruby to the uncle.

Once there, however, most of the building was boarded over. We peered through a gap in one of the boarded windows and saw no one inside. It looked as though the shop had been burgled. What had not been stolen was discarded haphazardly on the floor.

A man approached us from the store adjoining the Sheik's Treasures. He greeted us as he neared.

"A shame, sir. What they did to old Abdul. He was a good man. He was always kind to strangers, and fair with his customers."

"What happened here?" Barnwell demanded.

"It was a Sunday night, a few weeks back. Come Monday morning, it was obvious his store had been robbed. I went to his apartment to check on him. I received no answer to my knocks or calls, and I forced myself in only to find my friend dead on the floor. Such sadness."

The poor man standing before us was truly pained at the thought of his lost friend. Having heard the news, however, I began to fear a future pain: that of Mrs. Chodary.

"Condolences. Do you know what items were stolen?" Looking through the darkened window I saw quite a lot of merchandise still there. Pots, textiles, curious devices whose purpose was obscured by the dim light. The merchandise, however, was scattered as if the thief had been looking for … something. The ruby perhaps?

"Was there anything of particular value kept there, do you know?"

"I don't know exactly. Abdul never spoke much about business with me."

"Was Mr. Abdul a real Sheik?"

"Oh, Heavens no," the merchant said with a throaty laugh. "Abdul simply thought the mystique of the name and the color of his skin would encourage the curious to spend their money."

"And his associate?" asked the captain. "The tall sheik with a large white beard—can you tell me of him?"

"His associate, sir? There was no one. Abdul lived and worked alone. Nicest person in the world, but regarding business, he was a one-man show."

The captain asked, "Was Mr. Abdul a tea drinker?"

"More of a coffee drinker, I'd say. Always had a pot of his nasty Turkish coffee. Hardly an ounce of water topped by a gallon of coffee. Quite impossible to drink for my tastes." The man laughed. "I don't remember him ever drinking anything but that nasty stuff."

The captain and I shared a glance. The worry in his eyes told me everything. We gave the kind merchant a curt, but polite goodbye.

❧ 12 ❧

"The second Sheik," said Captain Barnwell after we left the merchant's presence. "He's the connection."

"Don't you think it strange this second Sheik would murder a fellow Arab, sell the ill-begotten goods, dress in a manner quite striking, and then spend several weeks meeting with the man to whom he sold the stolen items? I do not think we are dealing with an Arab or an old man."

"You told me the hotel clerk's description of the old man. He was seen by hotel workers a great deal."

"Yes, but not at his arrival or his departure. Sometimes, my friend, the most outlandish costumes provide the most natural cover."

"The nephew, then?"

I nodded, confessing my inner thoughts. "If the uncle's death was unnatural, the nephew is the only Clarkesville connection with motive and access."

"I admit, with the inheritance he had a motive, but he's a youth! A mere child. How could he possibly impersonate a sixty-year old sheik? It would require a great deal of knowledge of Arabic culture to fool an astute student of the world as was his uncle. Then there's the fact, he would have to trick his own kin—people who knew him—into believing a lie. I simply do not see it."

I thought of the few times the nephew had, in a masterful moment, altered his outward emotions as skillfully as any actor of great renown. It had impressed upon me his remarkable ability to affect complete control of his body. He was a youth, yes, but one with considerable learning and a taste for things foreign.

I took the captain by the arm.

"You may be right, Captain. But even so, you must return at once. I fear for Mrs. Chodary's life. Go to her and make sure she is in her right mind. If she acts in a strange manner, even in the slightest, immediately send her to Doctor Morgan and tell him it may be the effects of henbane. Whatever you do, keep her from her nephew."

"Do you have evidence beyond a motive? He is barely twenty years old."

"If I'm correct, I'll return shortly by train with the evidence. If I'm wrong, we may be looking at all this from the wrong angle. But please, to Mrs. Chodary. You may be her only hope."

The captain nodded and moved with haste to his carriage.

After my last interview at Clarkesville, the most fruitful and frightening of the day, I returned with haste to find Captain Barnwell sitting on a bench near Portia's Treasures. He had situated himself near enough to the shop to see its door, but far enough that no one inside could see him.

"Mrs. Chodary is not at the store according to the nephew," the captain said, frowning. "Young Mennell escorted me out and locked the door behind me. It being Sunday, I had not cause to remain. I have been watching the door since then."

"Good man, but I fear she is inside and suffering under her nephew's care. I will engage the youth and keep him from leaving. Go quickly. Get more officers and bring weapons."

"So, it was the nephew, then?"

"I am quite certain."

Captain Barnwell nodded and ran to his carriage. I yelled after him, "And do have someone call for Dr. Morgan."

I adjusted my suit jacket and made my way to the store.

❧ 14 ❧

Entering the building, I saw the nephew through the opened door of the backroom. He was hurriedly gathering select items and shoving them into a bag.

"Your aunt, where is she?"

He was startled when he saw me standing inside the shop. He knew he had locked door. Using a trick the famous Alfred C. Hobbs had once taught me, I had, quietly and quickly, engaged the tumblers of that simple lock and entered without his knowledge.

"S-She is out for a delivery at the moment, I believe."

He shoved the bag out of sight behind the counter and hurried to my location. He took me by my arm, and tried to nudge me toward the door.

"Didn't I lock...? Never mind." His bewildered expression was replaced by a look of determination. "It is Sunday. We are not open today. Furthermore, I have an appointment."

"An interesting habit you have, of always leaving as I arrive."

He grunted as I jerked my arm from his grip.

"I see you have tea prepared." I said, nodding at a teacup

on a table near the stairs. "Is it perhaps Mr. Campbell's leaves?" I suspected he had not brewed it for himself. "Or perhaps, the Sheik's leaves?"

His face darkened. "I really must insist you leave now."

I looked about the room until my eyes fell upon the aunt's cane. When she first approached me at the *Agora*, she had the same cane, and every time I had seen her walk, she had used it. She relied on that cane. I doubted she would have left the shop without it.

The teacup. The cane. I feared the worst, but I needed to keep Mennell occupied until Captain Barnwell returned. Mennell was physically stronger than I, and I was unarmed.

"I smell a hint of jasmine in the air. It is a most delightful scent. Do you not agree?"

He moved, once again, trying to forcibly nudge me out the door.

I stood my ground and said, "I understand you wish to be an actor."

The nephew looked up with large eyes, his cheeks slightly flushed. "Who told you that?"

"Actually, it was quite a coincidence. I had some business in Clarkesville and happened to meet an old friend. I mentioned your uncle's sad passing. He is a dean at Mount Solace—I believe that was your school—and when he heard your uncle's name, he asked if you were a relation."

"I...I wasn't there very long."

"No, you weren't, but it was long enough to create quite an impression on my friend."

A few moments passed in silence. Mennell had ceased nudging me toward the door. His face was stony; he appeared unable to reply.

Then, the stone cracked, and the young man smiled.

He moved back toward the counter. "Gone are those days," he said, waving his arms playfully. "The world may be a stage, but now my only desire is to help my poor aunt during this difficult time." His right wrist twirled with a flourish as he spoke. His motions indicated the fluidity and control of a seasoned actor, and he projected his voice up and over, as if on stage.

I had, in fact, met an old friend from Mount Solace. He was an actor himself and had become something of a mentor to young Chodary. He told me Mennell left after his mother's death. It was not out of grief, but from his desire to act and travel the world. Their deaths removed the parental restrictions which had prevented him from living out his dreams. The dean tried to persuade him to finish his education before traveling but Mennell was quite adamant about his intensions. My friend received the occasional letter from Mennell during the next two years which held accounts of his adventures as he traveled. The most important fact I learned, from the consultation with my friend, was Mennell's travels had lead him both to the Middle East and to remote Burma.

I nodded and walked to the counter as I weighed the information I had discovered that dreary Sunday morning. I understood what it all meant, but I needed to be cautious. I wanted to know whether I could use the subject of theater to draw out the time until Captain Barnwell et al arrived. If I played my hand too quickly, without the aid of the police, I would certainly be in danger.

I leaned close into the man, my elbows resting on the wood of the counter as my fingers tapped a rhythm.

"Most interesting. I have tried my hand at writing plays. Amateurish and entirely unsuitable for publication, of course, but the arts do transcend the mundane world, do you not agree?"

Mennel stole a nervous glance at my dancing fingers. His stony smile had returned, and a slight ripple moved through that hard countenance.

"The man that hath no music in himself," he said with a voice little more than a whisper, "nor is not moved with concord of sweet sounds, is fit for treasons, stratagems, and spoils."

"Quoth Lorenzo, I believe," I said, remembering my Shakespeare.

"Indeed." He smiled but took a step back, removing himself from my immediate presence. "You say you are an amateur playwright. Pray tell, let's have a summary of one of your plays."

I took my opportunity to extend the delay. "Well, as I said, I am a very poor playwright, but if you insist, I would be delighted."

Mennell nodded appreciatively while bowing slightly, his hands spreading wide in a welcoming gesture. He once again demonstrated, as an actor, his remarkable ability to instantaneously switch his true emotional state to a believable, but unfeeling facade.

I had one simple hope—that my own acting would suffice to allow the time for Captain Barnwell's arrival.

"Please," I said waving my hand toward a chair, "take a seat and I shall recount the basic plot of my latest work. I am immensely proud of it, but I must warn you, it does not have an ending. It is very much a work in progress."

He made a quick clapping motion with his hands and sat. He didn't say a word, but he looked at me, smiling and, apparently, eager to listen.

"I have titled it, 'Blood is Thicker than Water'."

His reaction to the title was a return of that stony smile, but within that smile, I noticed a slight fissure.

"It is a story of a man who suffers from an addiction. He is bright and quite talented, but his addiction drives him to commit extreme acts of evil—even murder. Yes, his addiction leads him to personal disaster."

"Oh, I do love a good murder mystery," the youth said with an utterly believable tone. "What sort of addiction ails him?"

"Gambling," I said and watched the smile drop. It rapidly reappeared as I continued to speak. "You see, he squandered great wealth in less than two years. His parents died at sea and left the young man a substantial fortune—large enough to sustain him for the rest of his life, were he but wise and prudent. As is said, however, the young rarely display either virtue. Very soon, the devil in the cards, so to speak, left him bereft of his inheritance or family to give him aid."

I paused. The smile was gone, but he retained the appearance of interest. I was making a few leaps in judgment based on what I knew, but I could be forgiven. This was my play, after all.

The nephew didn't speak. I cleared my throat and continued.

"That's not entirely true. The young man had an aunt and uncle in another city. They weren't money—not like the impoverished man's parents, but they lived well enough. He wanted their business for himself, but—and here is my twist —he approached his uncle in disguise."

"That's no good at all."

"It isn't?"

"No," he said, shaking his head. "No one would believe a nephew could fool his own uncle. Surely the uncle would know his mannerisms, tone of voice, colloquialisms, et cetera. I do realize this is for the stage, but one must present some modicum of reality."

"Quite right. As I said, it isn't a very good story, but I do have a reasonable explanation as to why the uncle would fail to recognize his nephew. First, although they only lived some thirty miles apart, the nephew almost never visited his aunt and uncle. On occasion they would exchange written correspondence, but they hadn't seen each other since his parent's funeral and before that, the nephew was too busy with school and acting to visit, even when the aunt and uncle came to town."

"But, surely, they would have recognized him."

"Ah, one would think, but I have seen amazing transformations afforded by minor concealments. For example, the lad in my play wears false facial hair, a hat, dark glasses, and is quite adept at mimicking other people's mannerisms."

"Forgive me, but I still do not see how his family would be fooled."

"Did not Odysseus test his family's loyalty by disguising himself as a beggar? I also gave the uncle of my play poor vision. Oh," I said, raising my eyebrows. "*Your* uncle also had poor eyesight, did he not?"

Did I notice a slight twitching in his right eye?

I continued. "In this play of mine, I do imply the young man was foolish for wasting his inheritance, but he was no fool. He traveled extensively and gained knowledge of the customs in many foreign lands."

I waited for him to speak.

"You don't have an ending yet, you said."

"I was hoping you might have a suggestion."

"A happy ending," he said curtly. "Perhaps he reconciles with his aunt and uncle and they live happily ever after. There. A culmination, with your moral theme of blood being thicker than water, completed."

"A most splendid suggestion." Waving my index finger high in the air, I added, "Oh, but I forgot one important detail. The nephew had already murdered his uncle."

Mennell narrowed his eyes.

"Why would he do that? You already said they did not have much money."

"Yes, but they had an established business which provided

a constant revenue. Oh, and I forgot to tell you. The young man only received half his inheritance which he had spent in his travels. The other half was held by his aunt and uncle until a time they deemed him worthy to receive it. So, he had a motive, you see. If he were able to dispose of them, he would have the business and the inheritance at once. This was the motive behind the disguise. Finally, the business provided the means by which he could sell the items he had stolen from the merchant he murdered prior to approaching his uncle. Ah, I forgot to mention that murder as well. Pardon my omission."

The nephew was silent for a few moments. "If I didn't know better, Mr. Brooke, I would reproach you for accusing me of some heinous deed. My uncle died of a natural cause. The police have so concluded."

I pointed to the table by the stairs. "You should finish your tea."

His silence told me the tea contained more than mere tea leaves. I walked toward the tea cup, leaned over it, and caught a hint of jasmine. The aroma confirmed my suspicions.

"You didn't brew that for yourself, did you? Where is your Aunt Portia?"

"I have already told you. She isn't here." The youth coughed into his fist and continued, "Ah, I do apologize, but the appointment I mentioned earlier..."

"Gold," I said as loudly as I could without overtly shouting. I hoped Mrs. Chodary, if conscious, would hear my voice and somehow respond. I quickly added, "Gold, silver, or lead."

"Pardon?"

"You mentioned Lorenzo. I'm speaking of the three suitors for Portia in Shakespeare's Merchant of Venice—the three suitors had to choose between those three objects. Gold, silver, or lead. The first of the suitors was the Prince of

Morocco, whom we might call a sheik. Like you, he chose the gold, the money. He chose poorly. He lost his chance at winning Portia."

At that moment, as if answering to her name, a subdued, but unmistakable moaning from upstairs reached my ears.

I took a hasty step forward and stopped. The nephew pulled an object from his coat pocket.

"Ah, but Mr. Brooke, you see, I have another chance to choose."

Mennell maneuvered around the counter. In his hand, he gripped a revolver.

"As you said, before the Prince were three caskets. Gold, silver, and lead." He smiled and aimed his weapon at my heart. "In the play, the Arabian prince may have chosen gold, but I, as the Sheik, I get my choice. I will thus win both Portia and you in one fell swoop. I now choose lead!"

"Y ou see, Mr. Brooke," the young man said as he kept his gun aimed at me. "My aunt said my uncle went to Clarkesville on business. That's not exactly true. Actually, he came to see me at my request."

"You demanded the remains of your inheritance, did you not?" I asked.

"Figures my aunt would tell you everything." He glared at me with a deep hatred I found unfathomable. "But no. I did not do that; I simply asked him for a loan. The thief, at least, owed me that much. I did not even demand for what was rightfully mine. Just a loan! But...but he said no." Mennell laughed. "So much for our familial bonds."

He traced the gun in a circular motion and laughed even harder.

"I left him," he said, continuing, "but not for good. I was about to return to him and force him to give me my money when the old Arab happened upon my uncle. The happenstance was truly fortuitous. I heard my uncle express some interest in what the man had to sell, but it was past sunset, and he asked the man to meet with him the next morning at the Clarkesville hotel in which he was lodging."

"I see. You met the Arab, Abdul, that evening. You killed him and thereafter posed as Abdul, knowing your uncle's eyesight was poor."

"Not exactly. It is true, my uncle's eyesight was poor, but he wasn't blind. If I had attempted to portray a man my uncle had just seen, it would have been difficult indeed—regardless how talented I may be as an actor. Besides, I didn't have time enough to study the Arab's accent and mannerisms. My uncle was no fool and I had to act fast. He would be returning home that next day."

"Ah," I said. "You posed as the second sheik, the merchant's phantom business associate."

The nephew nodded. "Indeed, I did!"

"You offered the goods the Arab had prepared, plus the ruby?"

"Yes. My uncle was a stingy man. He would have turned down the offer had I not showed him the ruby. I told him its worth and its history."

"But," I said, "you lied about its history."

Mennell stood silent.

"Did you steal the ruby from the Sheik, or was it during your travels? I feel it was the latter."

He remained quiet but added a smile.

"I see. One thing I do not understand. From my research, henbane is not addictive. How did you compel your uncle to return every night to you as he did?"

"Oh, I am quite capable of weaving a captivating tale of the macabre and esoteric. It's all nonsense, of course, but with the ruby and my uncle's foolish beliefs, it worked far beyond my hopes." Still smiling, he added, "When his interest in the occult wasn't enough, a bit of cocaine worked wonders on his mind. Now, up you go," he said, waving his hand and gun in the direction of the stairs. "Let's pay a visit to dear auntie. She's taken ill, I'm sad to say."

"I wondered why the killer allowed your uncle to retain the ruby those last weeks, but, as the nephew, you would only have to wait for the old man and woman to die before you took the ruby and the remainder of your inheritance. You were perfectly placed to steal his livelihood as well. This store is an ideal outlet for selling your ill-gotten goods. Quite clever."

The young man pointed upstairs with his gun. "I am sorry your play will be left forever unfinished. Go on, now. Upstairs."

I took my time walking to the stairs, hoping the captain would arrive before a bullet, but no one entered the shop. My only consolation was the knowledge I had left the front door unlocked and the youth seemed to have not realized that fact.

I stopped midway. Turning to face Mennell at the base of the stairs, I began, "I'm curious. How did you..."

Just then, a shadow flew across the window. Hoping the shadow belonged to Captain Barnwell, my eyes moved above and looked beyond the murderer. It was a momentary glance, a slight change of my expression, but Mennell followed my line of sight and looked to his side, toward the door.

The mere thought of what I did next makes my now aged self envious of those bygone years. Taking advantage of the distraction, I leapt from those stairs and hit my foe below.

The impact dislodged the gun from his hand and we fell to the floor, but the younger Mennell overcame the shock faster than I. He used his superior strength to push me away and recovered his feet before I could recover my thoughts.

As I scrambled to my feet, I found myself in front of the counter staring at Mennell. He had regained his gun and it was once again pointed at me.

"That's quite enough, Mr. Brooke. Upstairs. That is the

last time I'll tell you," he said, moving his gun in the direction of the staircase. "I'm not too keen on cleaning your blood off the merchandise down here, but I will if you do not move this instant. Besides," he said, suddenly smiling, "I think you'll enjoy what I have in store for you. We, and by that, I mean you, shall enjoy a tea party. The tea is of the highest quality, assured by the Grand Sheik of Mumbo Jumbo."

Mennell crumpled his eyebrows, and a deep, accented voice, which sounded remarkably like that of an old Arab, issued forth from the young man's lips.

"I will teach you the secrets of immortality. I can see many things impossible. You can fly!" At those last words, he let out a hearty laugh.

I backed up against the counter, my hands behind my back, feeling for what I hoped had not been moved.

And there it was: The Three Mystic Apes sitting beside the aunt's cane.

It was quite unfortunate the earlier shadow I had seen had not belonged to Captain Barnwell. Even still, I held to the hope that the captain would show soon.

"What is it about The Three Mystic Apes that bothers you so?" I asked. "You moved it specifically from the entrance."

"Don't be ridiculous," Mennell said, through a dismissive laugh. "It is an ugly piece of rubbish."

"See no evil; hear no evil; speak no evil."

"Bah! Go upstairs. Now!"

"What would your parents think of you at this moment?"

"I don't care what my father would think of me. He's nothing to me."

Interesting way to answer, I thought.

"But your mother, you do care what she would think. You removed, but did not get rid of, the three monkeys, because you see her watching you through their eyes, do you not?"

He was silent, but the gun remained aimed at my heart.

"The ties that bind—that blood be thicker than water, than all!"

"Shut up!" he shouted, his gun hand wavering ever so slightly.

"That is the song it plays, is it not? Your mother's favorite. You should know it well. I believe she often sang it to you when you were a child."

"I'm warning you..."

I continued with the lyrics. "For love doth find—that blood be thicker than water, than all!"

At that moment, my finger from behind my back flipped the switch of the music box. As the song began to play, I grabbed Mrs. Chodary's cane and swung.

He fired two shots, but neither were aimed at me.

The music had stopped as the cane found its mark into the back of Mennell Chodary's head. He dropped the gun, fell to his knees, and began massaging his injury. Retrieving the gun, I pointed it at him and firmly took control.

The shop door opened, revealing a disheveled and breathless Captain Barnwell together with four additional officers.

"Dear Lord, Carl, I heard multiple gun shots and thought the worst."

"Captain," I said, nodding toward the Three Mystic Apes on the counter. "I was not the victim."

Looking at the "see no evil" monkey, I frowned. It had been decapitated. The second shot had bored a large hole through the center of the music box, stopping the sound.

Doctor Morgon raced into the shop. "Upstairs. I heard her cry a few minutes ago. No doubt, she is heavily drugged. Quickly as you can, Doctor."

❦ 16 ❦

"I am eternally grateful for your diligence in this matter," Mrs. Chodary said from her bed at St. Matthews—a mere week after her nephew had been arrested.

"But of course, Madam. I am terribly sorry for the loss of your husband. I have come to the realization that he was a most interesting and intelligent man."

She nodded. "I must also thank you for believing me when, honestly, you had little reason to do so."

"I have found, Mrs. Chodary, that a woman's intuition should never be easily dismissed. However, there is one matter about which you were terribly wrong."

"What is that, Mr. Brooke?"

"The curse of the ruby, of course."

"Ah, yes. I suppose I was a bit taken by the events, but my husband always talked of such matters and, you see, with the circumstances..."

"Completely understandable and it was something Mennell had known and exploited. However, now we have exorcised the curse, the reason for your desire to 'cast it into the nearest body of water' has also been exorcised. Would you not agree?"

"I still do not want it."

"I took the liberty, in recent days, to have a friend examine the ruby," I said, holding up the box that held the wondrous gemstone. "At first glance, I had suspected it to be from Burma, and not India, as your nephew suggested. It has a purplish-red hue with deep saturation. These qualities indicated a Burmese origin.

"However, I was shocked to learn its name. It is the *Nga Boh* or 'Dragon Lord.' It is the ruby that rightfully belongs to the Crown Prince of Burma, His Majesty, Kanaung Mintha.

"Due to the embarrassing nature of losing a national treasure, the theft was not widely publicized. Captain Barnwell quietly made inquiries with the British consulate and just this morning, we received word confirming your ruby is indeed the Dragon Lord. The Crown Prince is offering a handsome reward for its safe return." I smiled before continuing. "My dear lady, you have your retirement in this box." I patted the top of the container and offered it to her.

"I..."

"My lady, it is the best possible solution. The Crown Prince receives his ruby and you will be awarded ten thousand dollars."

I do believe the color fled from the woman's face as she heard the sum.

Recovering, she said, "But sir, I have already given it to you. To take it back would be dishonest."

"Not in the least. You acted on information you had at the time. For me to accept the ruby now would be truly acting in dishonesty. The ruby is yours."

"I cannot thank you enough."

I nodded with happy relief and bade her a fond farewell.

As FOR THE YOUNG MAN, MENNELL, THE BRITISH REPORT had more to say. It confirmed what my friend, the dean, told me in Clarkesville. After his wide travels, the nephew had made his way to the imperial palace in Burma. Captain Barnwell's original missive had included a description of Mennell and, by that description, the errant nephew had been identified. The lad had impersonated an English baron and befriended the Crown Prince.

This led to the opportunity of the theft, which also involved the seduction of the Crown Prince's younger sister. Mennell had used all his considerable acting skills to convince her to take the ruby secretly as a form of dowry. Once he possessed the ruby, he fled to Clarkesville alone.

On a happier note, Mrs. Chodary had gifted to our club, in its entirety, the remaining half of Mennell's inheritance once the courts formally released it into her hands. At her request, we used the money to create a fund aiding a local orphanage. Through investments and careful planning, Mrs. Chodary's generous gift is even to this day benefiting the children of that orphanage.

Regarding Mr. Chodary's final words, "The Mad Sheik is not," it is still a mystery. Was the uncle trying to tell his wife their nephew was poisoning him? Or was the dying man stating his belief that the Sheik is not to blame? Regrettably, neither I nor Mrs. Chodary ever came to a clear or certain conclusion.

VOLUME 5: THE CAPTAIN'S PLAY

The Agora Mystery Series

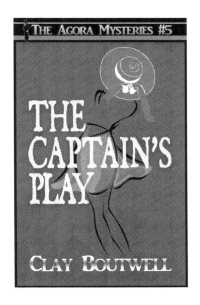

₰   I   ₰

June 15th, 1890

Carl Brooke
Boston

AFTER THE CHARLES TOCK AFFAIR, CAPTAIN BARNWELL
became an honorary member of the *Agora Society*. He often
reported on troublesome cases and asked for our expertise
and assistance. The members of our august society considered this both a public service and a form of mental exercise
among our members.

Even though our association with the Boston police was
extraordinarily interesting, we all took the captain's lectures
with the utmost seriousness. After all, being comprised of
professionals from varying fields of study, the *Agora Society*
had much to offer.

Also, as you will find in this current letter, he would occasionally pit our wits against the conclusions of his officers in relation to closed cases. One such episode, which I still retain the notes, occurred some years ago and is detailed in this letter.

I have entitled it, *The Captain's Play*.

⚜ 2 ⚛

The captain arrived precisely at six and our president, Christopher Harding, called the meeting to order. After a short word about a new library project, he motioned for Captain Barnwell to come forward.

The stoic officer did so with precise movement. He stood with a singular motion, and moved with a slow, but deliberate pace toward the podium.

Except when celebrating some extraordinary success or at play, my friend was always matter-of-fact and orderly with a remarkable control of his faculties. Every action or word seemed be a natural precursor to his next. "Clinical" would be a fitting word for him. On many an occasion, his stern and utterly logical disposition would drive a man—guilty or not—into confession and nervous prostrations.

His first lecture, delivered some months before the events in this letter, had been a tremendous success. Captain Barnwell's dry and understated delivery had left us unsuspecting as he deftly delivered his address with nail-biting suspense. No other speaker delighted our members quite like the captain.

On the night I am currently documenting, however, the

CLAY BOUTWELL

captain presented his talk in a different way. As the evening's designated scribe, I was prevented from offering many of my opinions and questions that night, but I have the record here as I write this letter. Limited only by the doubtful legibility of my shorthand, I believe the voices are fairly accurately presented.

According to my notes, twelve of us were in attendance that evening.

The principle characters included: engineer and architect Scott Lords, professor of theology John Hitch, the Renaissance scholar Anders King, watchmaker Edison Graves, printer Otto Snelling, and the practitioner of medicine Dr. Morgan.

Five other members attended that evening, but the aforementioned experts offered the bulk of the interactions in this present case.

I will use first names as was protocol during our little meetings, the only exception being Dr. Morgan. I have no clear recollection of why he alone was exempt, but it may have been because he was the personal physician to nearly all of us. Among our members, he was always "Dr. Morgan."

With a glass of water in hand, his mustache recently waxed, and his spectacles reflecting the light from a dozen strategically placed oil lamps, my friend, Captain Barnwell, moved in front of the podium and the captain's play began.

∗ 3 ∗

"**G**ood evening, gentlemen."
The captain, maintaining a serious posture, bowed slightly.

"It is my pleasure to once again come before you with a police matter that may be of interest to you."

Several members enjoyed a pipe, and they smoked whilst nestled deep into padded arm-chairs or on the club's beautiful mahogany sofa which had, as my mind pictures it now, a marvelous Grecian style. Others, the more studious amongst us, readied our pencils and papers for note taking. Whether anticipating an evening's entertainment or preparing for an education, we all gave Captain Barnwell our undivided attention.

"In previous lectures, I have endeavored to present before you the relevant facts of cases that have been troublesome to my detectives. On more than one occasion, input from the esteemed members of the *Agora Society* has aided the investigation. Furthermore, in at least one case, the *Agora's* contribution led directly to the apprehension of a murderer."

"Hear, hear!" Shouted Otto, the decidedly least reserved member of our little group. The rest of us clapped politely and softly lest we further fanned the flames of dear Otto's overabundant enthusiasm.

"However, with your permission this evening, my presentation shall take a new form."

The room quieted, the members keen to hear of this new form.

"A test of sorts," the captain said, continuing, a conspiratorial smile adding a twinkle to his gray eyes. "I will describe to you a concluded matter in which the Boston police force ultimately was successful in apprehending the criminal. The test, or puzzle if you prefer, will be for you, gentlemen, to piece together the truth as I state relevant facts. I will, of course, answer any questions you might have. I invite you to interrupt me at any time for queries no matter how trivial they may appear. As you know, very often the smallest of matters reveal the greatest of truths.

"The flow of the information tonight depends entirely upon your good selves. I will only say what we immediately observed and leave out what we deduced unless questioned directly."

The captain paused to sip his water and, I suspected at the time, to add dramatic pause to his performance. He set his glass upon the lectern and took a deep breath before continuing.

"This case occurred some years ago, but I will use false names as there are innocents still living today."

There were some scattered comments among us but all the whisperings were positive. The entire audience had great expectations for the entertaining night before us.

"Please do so, Captain Barnwell," said Otto. "Quite fun, I'd say."

Rubbing his hands together, the captain gave us the benefit of one of his rare smiles.

"Very well, let us begin."

$$\text{❦ 4 ❧}$$

"At precisely eleven o'clock in the evening a Mr. Jorge Gonzales of 621 Tremont Street, Boston, was aroused from his chair by the raised voices of a man and woman arguing just outside his door."

"How is it he knew the time exactly, sir?" asked Anders, after receiving a nod from the captain in response to his raised arm.

"He knew the exact time because, along with the voices, the long-case clock in his hallway chimed eleven times."

Anders nodded his thank you. The captain continued.

"The loud exchange outside was quickly replaced by the singular sound of the woman screaming. Upon opening his door, he spied two things. First, the fading figure of a screaming woman in a red dress fleeing into the distance. Second, the body of a dead man at Mr. Gonzales' doorstep. The dead man lay face down, and a knife protruded from his back."

The captain paused, meeting his severe eyes with each of ours. My friend's words and their dramatic delivery had a theatrical quality to them. Yes, I think this is a fitting comparison. Like an actor, the stalwart captain would carefully time his pauses to allow his listener's mind to process what had just been said and to speculate on what was to come.

"Now," said our narrator, "I must at this point take a moment to describe the scene in question. The part of Tremont Street on which Mr. Gonzales' home is located has several neighboring houses on both sides of the street. Any passerby on the street or neighbor looking out the window would no doubt have seen the body. A full moon shone bright in a cloudless night sky, and a newly-installed gas streetlight approximately two dozen feet from the body added its brightness to the scene. Both sources of light created a shallow, but consistent illumination over the entire front of Mr. Gonzales' house."

Otto shot up from his seat. The captain nodded and used the pause as an opportunity to take another sip of his water. On seeing the tumbler emptied, our president, the nearest person to the lectern, jumped up to refill it from the decanter set aside for the purpose. Again, our narrator nodded his thanks.

"What description did Mr. Gonzales give of the fleeing lady and of the body?" Otto asked and then sat down.

"Regarding the screaming and fleeing lady, the only identifying traits Mr. Gonzales could produce were the woman's attire. As already mentioned, the woman wore a bright red dress and a poke bonnet. The dress was notable in that it was cut quite low at the back. The bonnet had a small crown, but the brim was large, extending over the sides of her face. Mr. Gonzales further stated that the bonnet had two ribbons. One secured the bonnet to the chin and the other, for decorative purposes, circled the crown and trailed in the back some six inches or more. The ribbon matched the dress in redness as it flapped in the wind. There was, Mr. Gonzales reported, a brisk wind that evening.

"As to the corpse, he was a large man—perhaps two hundred and fifty pounds. The police discovered him in full evening dress with a top hat on the ground a few feet from his head, a silver-handled cane, and a glove on his right hand."

"A glove, singular?" asked Dr. Morgan, who remained seated in deference to his advancing years.

"That is correct, Doctor. A single glove. His right hand wore a kid glove of the palest hue. His left hand was bare. We did not find the missing glove in the vicinity."

"Odd," said Dr. Morgan. "A gentleman would of course remove his right-hand glove when greeting someone, but his left? And then to say it was not found in the vicinity?"

Captain Barnwell waited a few moments for another question. When none arrived, he continued.

"At this point, I would like to pause for your general assessment of the facts as I have so far reported them. What can you tell me of the situation?"

Scott raised his hand and the captain nodded, prompting the man to stand. "From the location at Tremont Street, the man's dress, and the time of night, we can assume we have a man returning from an evening at the theater."

"Yes, that was our thinking at the time."

"But with a missing glove," continued Scott. "Was there anything else odd about the man's dress? A mismatched sock, perhaps? A soiled handkerchief?"

"Yes. The right shoulder of the man's overcoat had smudges of what appeared to be red clay and yet he was found face down upon the cobblestones with no clay or any kind of dirt in the immediate vicinity. I will also say we found some stains on the man's vest and his white shirt. The stains were located around the upper chest region. We did not notice this until the outer clothing was removed the next morning during the post mortem."

"I see," said Scott. "And the glove on the right hand or the bare left hand, did either have clay markings similar to that found on the shoulder? And what about his knees?"

"No, sir. Left hand, glove, and both knees were all spotless."

"And the walking cane?"

"There was some clay of the same kind on the handle, but not on the ferrule attached to the bottom. Apart from the handle, the rest of the cane was spotless."

"What of the surrounding area where the body was found? Was that color of clay found anywhere near the body?"

"Nowhere near the body or along the street in front of the house, sir. However, the next morning, one officer did find a patch of clay matching that color in the lightly wooded area behind Mr. Gonzales' house. He also discovered a number of footprints in the area."

"Odd, wouldn't you say?" Scott said, tilting his head quizzically. "If the poor man had tripped and landed in a patch of dirt while fleeing from a pursuer, wouldn't he use his hands and knees to get back up?"

Captain Barnwell said nothing.

"Odder still that the cane had clay on the handle but not the base." Scott shook a puzzled look from his face and asked, "About the area behind the house, was it heavily trafficked?"

"No, sir. There were no roads or buildings nearby. It was nothing but darkened space."

Scott continued. "Did the footprints you found in the darkened space match the man's shoes? And how much of the clay was found on those same shoes?"

"The footprints did not match the man's shoes. They were smaller. Possibly the shoes of a child or a woman. The bottoms of the man's shoes were as spotless as the ferule of the walking cane. I must say at the time we were unable to determine if the footprints at the back of Mr. Gonzales' house had any relevance to the dead man located in the front of the house."

"Did you learn the identity of the dead man? And what articles did he have on his person?"

Captain Barnwell's eyebrows were level; his mustache covered his upper lip in such a way as to conceal the slightest emotional implication behind his words.

"As to your first question, no. At that moment, we did not have a name. Mr. Gonzales did, however, recognize the face as someone who frequented the theaters. The victim had nothing in his pockets but a ticket stub and a few half-dime coins. At that point, Mr. Gonzales woke his neighbors, one of whom set a manservant to summon the police. When we arrived at the scene, we noticed the few points I just mentioned: that the dead man had minor smudges of clay on his right shoulder and he carried no identifying articles on his person."

"Was Mr. Gonzales able to expand upon how he was able to recognize the dead man?" Scott asked and then sat.

"Mr. Gonzales worked as a stagehand at the nearby St. James Theatre and although he didn't know the victim personally, he had seen him a few times at the theater. Although the dead man was not an actor or a theater employee, Mr. Gonzales told us he had seen the man back-stage on more than one occasion. When we questioned him on what the man was doing backstage, he said with sudden enthusiasm, 'Ah! I know who the woman is.'"

Captain Barnwell took a moment for our minds to form the picture. Now, we were the detectives, trying to compre-hend the unsaid. He then lifted a piece of paper close to his eyes.

"Mr. Gonzales said, and I quote. 'Just now, sirs, I realized what was so familiar about that red dress. It wasn't just the bright red color, but the fact it was cut so low in the back. She bared her back for the world to see! Only Miss Vanderbilt would be so bold to wear such a dress. In fact, I saw her wearing that same outfit this very night at the theater. Not only that, but I saw this man twice backstage. Both times, he was in the east wing where the lead actors have their private rooms. One of those times, I saw him knocking on Miss Vanderbilt's private door. It was a number of weeks ago, but I'm positive he was the man. Miss Vanderbilt often wore a bright red dress and that matching hat and that is exactly the way I saw her tonight outside my window. It was her. I know it was her.'"

The captain looked up and awaited our questions.

"Did Mr. Gonzales see her face?" asked Scott.

"We asked that exact question." Captain Barnwell looked back down at his paper and said, "Here is what he replied, 'Well, no. She wore that closed bonnet, you see, but I am sure it was her. Miss Vanderbilt had caused something of a stir with that dress, she did. She was known for it. The fleeing woman had to be her. No lady would wear such a thing.'"

John raised a hand. Captain Barnwell signaled for him to speak.

"Did Mr. Gonzales know Miss Vanderbilt well?"

"No, not directly," Captain Barnwell answered. "He had never spoken with her. As a stagehand, his job involved moving props and managing the curtain weights. He had no direct interaction with the cast or patrons, but of course, he could often see those on stage and he saw Miss Vanderbilt regularly. She was, after all, an actress of some renown at that time."

"Did you ask Mr. Gonzales what he thought of Miss Vanderbilt?"

"He said she was a mean woman with a short-temper. She could be dismissive of the 'workers,' as she called anyone other than the lead actors. Apart from that, he had had no direct contact with the woman. He did say she had changed her stage name at least twice since he had been at the theater and had been 'Miss Vanderbilt' for only the previous three years. When asked what her real name was, he didn't know."

John nodded thoughtfully and Captain Barnwell cleared his throat.

"So, I would like to recapitulate the sequence of events thus far and to reframe it from the viewpoint of the police.

"We arrived at the scene of the murder around half past eleven which was approximately thirty minutes after Mr. Gonzales heard the screaming. A crowd of people had gathered, but the victim's body had not been touched. Once we removed the spectators, we examined the area more closely with our lanterns. At the corner of the house, we found a small patch of garden dirt that did not match the clay found on the victim's right shoulder, but in the dirt, we did discover some markings that ran diagonally for nearly two feet until the dirt hit the cobblestone.

"Furthermore, the relevant facts garnered from Mr. Gonzales were that he believed the woman he had seen fleeing the crime to be the actress Miss Vanderbilt. He was quite certain of it, although he did not see her face on account of the peculiar hat she wore and the direction she was fleeing. Also, on at least one previous occasion, Mr. Gonzales witnessed the victim knocking on the actress' door.

"At this point, I would like to open up the proceedings for questions or comments."

I hurriedly finished recording the captain's words and looked up. Every member had his eyes locked upon my friend.

5

Doctor Morgan stood. Captain Barnwell conceded the floor with a slight bow.

"Can you comment on the location of the knife in the man's back and describe generally the area surrounding the wound?"

"The blade of the knife was about four inches long. Approximately two inches of it was buried into the man's back, just under his right shoulder blade. It appears it had been the second stabbing attempt, the first being directly over the right shoulder blade."

"And of the amount of blood around the wound?"

"Very little. Of course, at the time we found him, he was wearing multiple layers of clothing including an overcoat, a swallow tail jacket, a vest, and a shirt. However, later, when the medical examiner removed the clothing, it was peculiar how little blood had stained his white shirt."

"Then," said the doctor, "what killed him?"

"A knife in the back isn't good enough?" asked Otto, crossing his arms and giving us all a very unsatisfied look.

"There are no major organs or blood vessels that a two-

219

inch deep knife would imperil. The blood had already clotted to an extent that only a few drops seeped out when the man was stabbed. Clearly, the man was dead prior to being impaled with the knife." The doctor turned his attention to Captain Barnwell. "Is this what your men concluded?"

"Yes, indeed. Once the body had been removed to the morgue and disrobed, the technician thought the limited blood stains unusual enough to alert us to that fact. We had a doctor examine the body and he concluded just as you said."

"Did you find any other stab marks or external wounds such as head trauma that might have caused the man's death," asked the doctor.

"Once examined closely, no. The only physical marks on the body were the two aforementioned stabbings. One shallow mark on the right shoulder blade and a second where the knife was found, just under the right shoulder blade."

Taking advantage of a pause in the captain's speech, Dr. Morgan said, "Given the circumstances, we must assume the man did not die a natural death, but I can conclude the knife wasn't the cause. If the knife did not kill him and there were no other external wounds, something he ingested perhaps did. Were there any signs of poisoning?"

"That was our suspicion, but at that moment we saw no obvious signs as to what it could have been."

The doctor relaxed back into his arm chair and rebuilt the fire in his meerschaum.

❦ 6 ❦

"Let's now turn our attention to the actress," said the captain. "With the aid of Mr. Gonzales, we were able to locate Miss Vanderbilt in short order even though it was past midnight by this time.

"She had retired for the night to her apartment which was a five-minute walk from the St. James Theatre. With the apartment manager's aid, she was awoken and once she had changed from her nightgown, she came with us to the station. There, we asked of her movements that evening. She claimed to have gone straight home after the night's final performance which ended at ten-thirty."

Otto stood, and the captain flashed a hand in his direction.

"Can you describe Miss Vanderbilt's general appearance?"

"She is a tall woman of about five feet and ten inches. Slight in build, she has blonde hair which she wore in a short-cropped style, modern to the period. Her age at the time was twenty-eight."

Otto asked, "What was her disposition at having been taken to the station?"

"Quite frankly, she was not at all pleased and didn't mind letting us know of her displeasure. It was after midnight and by every indication, she had already retired. We didn't tell her immediately the reason for our questions as we wanted to observe her reaction. But once we took her to the morgue and asked her to identify the dead man, her anger changed into complete grief. She cried inconsolably for some time.

"Once she calmed down, she said the following, and I quote, 'Yes, that is Mr. Lewis. How is it possible? I only saw him earlier tonight.' When asked of the reason for their recent contact, she said, 'Only this very day, I discovered that Mr. Lewis was married. Of course, I confronted him with the note and instead of explaining, he immediately left and without a word. That was the last I saw him.' End quote."

When Captain Barnwell looked up from the papers on the lectern, John asked, "The note?"

"An anonymous letter of a single sentence, typed and unsigned. It said Mr. Lewis was a married man. I have it here."

The captain held out a page for all to see. One of us took the paper, examined it, and passed it around.

To my eye, I saw nothing of particular interest. As the captain had said, it was a typed message consisting of a single sentence: "Mr. Lewis is a married man." I could see nothing special about the paper nor the wording. The only thing of interest was the fact it had been typed and left unsigned, clearly to disguise the person's handwriting.

"Did you ask about the red dress?" said John.

"Yes," replied the captain. "She admitted to having worn it that evening as Mr. Gonzales had stated, but she also claimed to have changed out of it and left it in her dressing room before returning to her home. We later found the dress exactly where she said it would be."

"And the hat?" John asked.

"The hat was there too. I will mention one peculiarity. The red ribbon attached to the hat had been torn and a section about three inches in length was missing."

Anders stood. "Was the torn piece of ribbon later discovered near the scene of the murder?"

"Yes, it was. There was an elm tree positioned between Mr. Gonzales' house and his neighbor's. The piece of fabric was found six feet from the ground, caught on a low hanging branch."

Anders asked, "Captain, we know Miss Vanderbilt was a stage name. Did you learn her real name?"

"Martha Simmons, but she insisted quite firmly we only refer to her as Miss Vanderbilt."

"One final question for the moment," said Anders. "Did you ask if anyone else had access to her dressing room? Did it have a lock?"

"Yes, on both accounts. She said she had only given the key to one person and that was Mr. Lewis."

"But the key was not found on Mr. Lewis' body, is that correct?"

"That is correct. The key was not found anywhere during our investigation."

Anders sat, and the captain continued. "When Miss Vanderbilt confronted Mr. Lewis that evening, she told us he had simply left quite upset that she had learned his secret. After that, she retired to her apartment, quite alone."

Scott raised a hand. "Were there any witnesses who saw Miss Vanderbilt enter her apartment?"

The captain shook his head. "There were none. We only have her word."

He paused and scanned the room to make sure no one else had any questions.

"Right. At this point, we had a name for the deceased and knowledge of a wife.

"We tracked down Mrs. Lewis and broke the news to her a little after two in the morning. The Lewis residence was on a farm well outside the city—some six miles from the theater. At age thirty-nine, she was quite a few inches shorter than Miss Vanderbilt, perhaps five feet three, and significantly wider in girth. She had long black hair that touched her lower back. Her immediate reaction was a silent shock and then, as Miss Vanderbilt had also done, she began to cry inconsolably.

"She eventually told us she suspected there had been another woman, but simply could not believe it to be true. When asked what made her suspicious, she said how her husband would often go out without her and he would not return home until the early hours. She admitted to hating the theater and refusing to go with him. And yet, in recent months, her husband had left her at home and visited the theater at every opportunity, despite their dwindling resources. When asked if the name Martha Simmons or her stage name, Miss Vanderbilt, meant anything to her, she simply stared into the distance, shaking her head."

Captain Barnwell rested his elbows on the lectern and, looking at his audience, he asked, "Now, gentlemen, other than the dead man, we have three principle characters in our plot. For the purpose of tonight's game, I will tell you that one of the following committed the murder: A, Miss Vanderbilt, the actress. B, Mrs. Lewis, the dead man's wife, or C, Mr. Gonzales, the man who discovered the body."

He paused, once again organizing his papers. All twelve of us gave the captain our rapt attention.

"Gentlemen, I have presented before you the relevant details exactly as we, the police, discovered them that evening and the following morning. So, now I ask you, who was the murderer?"

✷ 7 ✷

The left side of the captain's mustache twitched slightly, a physical sign of his apparent satisfaction in the performance of his play thus far.

"I wish for you now to ask questions. Through your questions, you will direct our little investigation until its conclusion. If there is some detail we did not ourselves investigate, I will simply tell you so."

Otto raised an excited hand. "At this point, the actress does seem to be the prime suspect. Was her changing room in the theater searched since it was a known meeting place between her and Mr. Lewis?"

"Yes. Immediately after speaking with Mrs. Lewis, we did indeed search the actress' dressing room. Upon opening the door, we were met with the strong odor of vinegar. Indeed, a bottle of vinegar was found near the door.

"We walked in and took note of what we saw. It was a small room about eight foot by sixteen, with two doors, one door from the theater hall from which we had entered and one to the outside, which had once been an access to an outhouse. The outside door was bolted and chained shut from the inside."

"Was there any indication the back door had been recently opened?" asked Anders, standing.

"It was possible, but we saw no obvious indication it had been. All we knew for certain, someone would have had to lock and chain the door from within the room."

"Thank you," said Anders.

"There was a table with a large mirror attached, a cot for sleeping, and a trunk with her clothes and other personal items. On the table, we found two tea cups. One empty and the other half full. The actress later denied having set those out or making the tea. A chemist was able to find in the empty cup traces of arsenic and other chemicals consistent with rat poison.

"Inside the trunk, at the bottom under her clothes, we found two objects of particular interest to the case. A white left-handed Kashmir glove that matched the glove Mr. Lewis wore when he was found. We also discovered a small box of opened Hammond's Rat Cake Poison. Again, the actress denied owning or having seen either of those items."

Edison stood and said, "Because you are here, and you would never present a case with such an obvious conclusion, it is clear that the actress has been framed and is not the murderer."

"Ahh," said the captain. "But you see, I know of your intelligence and perhaps I suspected you might be led to believe as such. I could very well be anticipating you brilliant gentlemen overthinking matters. Could it be, my friends, that I have come here to give you a most plain case masked to be misconstrued as something deeper?"

I smiled.

"Even still," said Edison, "the actress didn't do it."

"How so?" asked the captain.

"I'm a watchmaker by trade. I take in my hands a time-piece. I turn it over, open up the back, and I can see screws, springs, and wheels. I immediately recognize the meaning behind each part. But, even if I were not a watchmaker, I would still understand that each part had been designed and carefully positioned in a way to affect a desired outcome. Likewise, in this evening's story, all the gears, wheels, and weights are laid out to point toward the actress. Everything. It was intended to be so."

"Perhaps she acted in haste, murdered the man who had lied to her, and then retreated into shock, not being able to think of how to cover up her crime?" Otto suggested.

"Could she really have been such a brilliant assassin and then such a fool afterward?" retorted Edison to Otto. "Remember how the captain described the actress at first. She was angry at being inconvenienced at such a late hour. A person unable to think due to a traumatic experience wouldn't be able to pretend to be angry when interrogated by the police; she would instead sink inward, finally revealing her actions."

"She is an actress," I added.

Edison pouted his lips and faced Captain Barnwell.

"The flamboyant red dress with a unique low-cut back and the hat with the ribbon might make sense if the murder happened at that location and acted suddenly in the heat of the moment. Yes. But it would equally make sense as a way to frame Miss Vanderbilt while the bonnet concealed the killer's face. We've already established the man was not killed by the knife. Also, by the clay stain on his overcoat, I daresay he was not killed in front of Mr. Gonzales' house, either. The arsenic and empty teacup further suggest this."

"Ah, yes," said John. "All these items would imply the murder was planned and some effort was required."

"Precisely," said Edison. "Now, if Miss Vanderbilt was the

murderer, and she managed to plant the body—quite preposterous considering the size of the man—why in the world would she wear her peculiar red dress and hat—something she was known for owning?"

"But if you are suggesting," said Otto, "that the wife murdered her husband and then moved the body to the location where it was later found, we would have an even greater problem on our hands. I would remind you that Mrs. Lewis is an even smaller woman than the actress."

After a few moments of silence, John stood.

"Just one moment," he said, raising a hand. "I remembered something the captain said early on. There were two voices, that of a man and a woman arguing before the woman in the red dress screamed and fled alone. How then, could the murder have been committed elsewhere?"

Once again, the room was silent. After finishing writing my shorthand for John's last words, I stood, using the silence as a chance to speak.

❧ 8 ❧

"So, we have four players: three possible suspects and one dead victim.

"Perhaps, it was Miss Vanderbilt who, having heard the man she loved was married, lashed out in anger and killed her lover—although admittedly, poisoned tea would require some planning. But regarding the problem of the two voices, as an actress, I have no doubt she would be used to speaking with different styles of voices including mimicking that of a man. All this would leave us with the sole question that Edison posed: why would she leave so many clues pointing to herself?"

I took a moment to gauge the reaction of the members. Unless I badly misjudged their faces, except for Edison, most seemed quite convinced it was the actress and that was that. I continued.

"Or perhaps it was Mrs. Lewis who, also upon learning of her husband's infidelities, decided to kill him. I do not think it inconceivable that even a woman untrained in the theater could disguise her voice and be taken as a man through a series of walls by the half-asleep ear of Mr. Gonzales. Or perhaps," I said, continuing, "it was Mr. Gonzales who secreted a love for Miss Vanderbilt and saw the killing of Mr. Lewis as a way to get closer to the actress. An introduction and *déclaration d'amour* by way of police, you might say. Naturally, the problem of hearing two different people would disappear as the voices would simply have been a lie to turn attention away from himself."

Otto stood. "If it wasn't Mr. Gonzales and the murder took place away from his residence, it seems doubtful either woman could carry a two hundred and fifty pound man," said Otto, crossing his arms.

"Then," said John, "it was Mr. Gonzales. He alone could have moved the dead man. Perhaps he only had to move him a few feet after murdering Mr. Lewis from within his house. Also, as a stagehand, he had ready access to all rooms in the theater, thus able to plant the glove and poison at ease."

"But," said I, "framing her undermines our only motive: that he was infatuated with Miss Vanderbilt and wanted to remove his competition."

"Yes, that it does," John admitted. "Unless she had rejected his advances with scorn and he wanted both Miss Vanderbilt and her lover to suffer. He himself described her as a rough individual. I do not think this scenario implausible."

I nodded and then turned toward the captain. "At this point, I have but one question. Did the neighbors also hear the conversation and the screaming and did anyone else see the fleeing woman?"

"Three residents of the nearest houses reported hearing the screaming and one said she thought there were multiple people outside. She did not, however, speculate on either the gender or the content of the conversation. Another even saw the woman briefly as she fled down the street and into the darkness. As Mr. Gonzales had stated, this neighbor describes the fleeing woman as wearing a flashy red dress with a low cut back and a bonnet with a long red ribbon flapping behind her."

"There we go," I said. "A corroboration that at least supports if not exonerates Mr. Gonzales. If we weren't playing a game, I would entertain the thought that Mr. Gonzales had one or more accomplices. But we have already been told one of these three is the murderer."

"But could Mr. Gonzales still have committed the murder and deposited the body for a random pedestrian who happened to be wearing that red dress to discover it?"

"I think not," I said. "Do not forget the piece of ribbon that was found in the alleyway next to Mr. Gonzales' house. It matched the ribbon of the actress' bonnet and was found on the side of the house, not along the street in the front. The fleeing woman had most certainly come from behind the house, presumably with the body. The woman who fled wore the red dress and hat belonging to Miss Vanderbilt. But, even if the torn ribbon could be explained away, to have such a woman in the same area that Miss Vanderbilt was known to haunt and to appear at the right time, seems a little coincidental. Remember what Mr. Gonzales said, 'Miss Vanderbilt had caused something of a stir with that dress.' She was known for it."

"Then you are suggesting the wife did it."

"She had a motive," said I. "A cheating husband who both wasted their finances and their marriage. And consider the missing key Miss Vanderbilt gave her husband. Perhaps she discovered the key and used it to plant the evidence in Miss Vanderbilt's dressing room."

"The key," said Otto. Turning to the captain, he asked, "You say the key was never discovered?"

"I'm afraid not. It appears the killer discarded it."

"I see. You've described the wife as shorter and heavier than the actress," said Edison. "Captain, in your opinion, having examined the dress and set eyes on both women, do you think the wife could have worn it?"

Captain Barnwell said, "On close examination, no. It would be obvious the dress was not hers. The dress would have been too long for her height and too tight for her waist. However, if you are asking if she could have worn it to be seen at a distance, I believe so—especially with the closed bonnet hiding the bulk of her face."

"Still, whether it was the actress or the wife, one problem remains. If it wasn't the man," said Edison, "how could a woman possibly carry the weight of a fully grown dead man some distance?"

"Captain Barnwell," said John, "please describe in detail the markings you found in the patch of dirt at the corner and those found in the clay behind Mr. Gonzales' house?"

"On the corner garden area at the front of the house—a small patch perhaps three by four feet—was found a single two-inch wide tire track running diagonally across. In the larger area behind the house, of grass and dirt, we found footprints of a smallish sized shoe. It appeared the person was trying to avoid leaving tracks by staying as much as possible on the grass, but it is also obvious someone had recently made an impression in the grass and dirt. Furthermore, there is a larger area of disturbed clay perhaps two feet from the tire track in the back. All I'll say here is the color of that area matched the color of the clay found on Mr. Lewis' right shoulder. The size and shape are what you might expect to see from a body falling on his shoulder."

"Ah," said I, "you give us too much."

"I only say what we immediately saw—although we didn't notice what I just described until the next morning. I will not say whether the tire track or footprints have any final relevance to the case. However, I will say this. At the time we saw some significance to them as they appeared to have been freshly laid."

The captain had led us through two acts of his play. Had the curtains closed at that moment and forced a response from me, I would have felt certain in my conclusion. Still, I remained silent; the pieces I had gathered together were telling, but not absolute.

John stood and said, "Let us dwell on this theory a moment: that the footprint was left by the murderer, one of the two women by the footprint size. She then used some mechanism with a single tire—perhaps a wheelbarrow—to move the much heavier man from where she had killed him, either the theater or some other location, to the front of Mr. Gonzales' house.

"On the way, going through the lightly wooded area behind Mr. Gonzales' house, she stumbled in the dark and the body and cane spilled out from the wheelbarrow. It fell into the grass and, more importantly, onto the red clay. Once recovered, she quietly deposited the body in front of Mr. Gonzales' house and then removed the wheelbarrow to the darkness behind the house. Returning to the body, she affected male and female voices and then screamed while stabbing the dead man. She did so in haste, first hitting bone before finding purchase beneath the man's right shoulder blade.

"In this scenario, it is clear the murderer planned the discovery of the body well in advance. Clearly, this means the murderer was not the actress, but someone who wanted to implicate the actress. If the actress would have thought of all this but forgot to change her bright red dress which identified her to any regular theatergoer, it would not be consistent with an otherwise well-considered and executed plan. Add to that the obviously planted items: the teacups, the poison, and the missing glove, and we have someone wishing to implicate the actress."

"Yes, and going by our dwindling list of possible suspects, the murderer was the wife. In this line of thinking, Captain," Anders said looking up from his notes, "could you explain to us what your investigation did regarding the wife? Also, could you tell us your impression of her when confronted?" Anders readied his pencil and stared expectantly at the captain.

The captain had been smiling, clearly enjoying the excitement and conversation his theatrics had caused.

I was, likewise, thoroughly enjoying the evening. No doubt every man in the room was trying to identify the murderer. All three suspects had the opportunity and, to some degree, all three had a motive, at least potentially. I looked around the room; in my colleagues' eyes, there was not one single hint of boredom. I only saw faces of concentration and interest.

The captain cleared his throat once more. "About the wife, gentlemen, when we interrogated her the next day, one queer thing was her quickness to point the finger at Miss Vanderbilt. Still, she did seem genuinely in pain as a result of both her husband's infidelity and his untimely death. I have here the transcript of our interview with Mrs. Lewis, which we conducted the day after his body was discovered. A moment, please."

The captain shuffled his papers and once satisfied he had found the relevant document, said, "Ah, here we go."

With your indulgence, I shall now present the police

interview in the manner Captain Barnwell delivered it to us that evening—as though it were a play script.

POLICE: HOW LONG WERE YOU MARRIED.

Mrs. Lewis: Ten years this April, sir.

Police: And how often did your husband visit the theater without you?

Mrs. Lewis: All the time recently. I would never go. Jezebels like that Miss Vanderbilt infest such places.

Police: You knew of Miss Vanderbilt, did you?

Mrs. Lewis: Well, no. But you had already mentioned her name and I just assumed she was the killer.

Police: We never make assumptions so early in our investigations, Ma'am.

Mrs. Lewis: Of course.

Police: Your husband was found with only one white glove. Do you have any idea where the other glove could be and why he only had one?

Mrs. Lewis: Of course. That makes sense.

Police: What makes sense, Mrs. Lewis?

Mrs. Lewis: Do you not know of the tradition of a male theatergoer giving a favorite actress one of his evening gloves? Again, it had to be her. I bet you'll find that missing glove with her.

Police: I see. You say you didn't go to the theater at all? How do you know of such a tradition?

[There was a long pause before Mrs. Lewis proceeded.]

Mrs. Lewis: I used to go as a young woman, you see. Well, I might as well tell you. I hesitate to mention this because it is not the woman I am today. I was once an actress myself. I spent many years in that world of degradation. It's how I met my husband, you see. I even received his glove one night, but...I have given up that life of sin, sir.

Captain Barnwell set down the page. "Gentlemen, I wanted to read that passage from our interview since it gave us a reason behind the gloves and a possible connection with the theater. Incidentally, this was before we had discovered the glove in the trunk of the actress. Any questions regarding Mrs. Lewis?"

Otto stood. "It is quite interesting that not only did she know of a tradition which would explain her husband's missing glove, but also suggested, correctly, where it might be." He looked toward the watchmaker. "One of your springs and wheels, perhaps, Edison?"

Edison nodded. "Indeed. Quite a large wheel, I'd say." He stood and turned to the captain. "I have a question regarding Mrs. Lewis."

The captain dipped his head in Edison's direction.

"She stated she had once been an actress—through which she had met her husband—but had forsaken that lifestyle. Did you perhaps interview neighbors or friends to corroborate those statements?"

"Yes, we did," replied my friend, smiling. "They all said she was an exemplary citizen and her husband didn't deserve her. One neighbor in particular said she would often visit Mrs. Lewis to comfort her when that, and I quote, 'low-life husband of hers' was gone to town. When asked, this neighbor said she had been with Mrs. Lewis until nine o'clock the evening of the murder, which would make it difficult, but not impossible for Mrs. Lewis to have committed the crime. Not quite a solid alibi. A sister living in Boston stated Mrs. Lewis had indeed once been a starlet actress of the stage but had since become a totally different person. While once an actress of some fame and accomplishments on stage, she, according to the sister, had also been a terrible drunk. One day, she gave up the bottle and suddenly left the theater never to return."

"Thank you, sir. One more question. She stated she didn't know Miss Vanderbilt, but had she at any time seen Miss Vanderbilt outside the theater? I mean, could she have recognized her?"

"She denied knowing of the actress during our initial questioning, but later in the investigation, we showed Mrs. Lewis a program booklet with an etching of Miss Vanderbilt's likeness. Once we again mentioned Miss Vanderbilt's real name, Martha Simmons, she seemed to faintly recognize her as someone she may have known a decade earlier. She stressed she couldn't be certain, however."

"Thank you, Captain. Next, I'd ask Miss Vanderbilt if Mr. Lewis said anything about his wife or if she had had any personal contact with her."

"She said she had no idea Mr. Lewis was married until that very evening, but when asked if she knew who the wife was, she immediately said she had heard of her. Miss Vanderbilt claimed Mrs. Lewis was a 'busybody,' as she called her, who was always around the theater causing trouble. She also said that it was no wonder Mr. Lewis thought her such a horrible woman for her prudish self-righteousness."

Otto stood. "If she had heard of the last name 'Lewis' how come she didn't know Mr. Lewis was married."

"We did ask that," said the captain. "She said it was a common name and she simply did not make the connection."

At this point, I stood. The captain looked in my direction and nodded.

❧ 10 ❧

"**I** would like to make absolutely clear one piece of information that is critical to our correct understanding of the events as they occurred," I said, addressing my fellow amateur detectives. "Was the man killed in front of Mr. Gonzales' house or was it done elsewhere. And if elsewhere, where exactly? Relevant facts, gentlemen."

The doctor stood. "In my medical opinion, the man had been dead some time before he was stabbed. As to how long, it is hard to say. Perhaps an hour, maybe longer."

"Clearly," said Otto. "A body would not have been left out in the open for over an hour and remain undiscovered, even at that late in the evening. The captain previously described the area as being residential and fairly well-lit. I would suspect it is more likely for the killer to have been the screaming woman or else someone who had deposited the body moments before the screaming woman arrived."

John said, "But at that time of night, eleven o'clock, you said. Were there any passersby?"

"That is unknown," said the captain. "However, people

leaving the theater could have conceivably walked right past the front of Mr. Gonzales' house."

"I believe," said I, "barring a resurgence in doubting Mr. Gonzales' innocence, the screaming woman was indeed the murderer."

"How so?" asked Otto. "I still think she could have simply been a woman who happened upon the body."

"Mr. Gonzales believed it was the actress Miss Vanderbilt and a neighbor corroborated the fact the fleeing woman wore that distinctive red dress and the hat with a flowing red ribbon. We've established that only Miss Vanderbilt would have worn those two very distinctive articles. A piece of the ribbon was found in the alley where only the killer would have travelled. How certain," I asked Captain Barnwell, "are you that the torn ribbon was from the bonnet?"

"It was a perfect match, sir."

"Since others witnessed the fleeing woman, it follows, therefore, Mr. Gonzales is utterly innocent in this murder unless you believe there could have been another woman, in the vicinity and on that night, dressed in a similar fashion and just happened to have travelled through the alleyway and then had mistakenly deposited her bonnet with the torn ribbon in the actress' dressing room."

"If that particular dress and hat," said Otto, "could only have been the actress' dress and hat, then the murderer would have to be one of the women, the only two with potential access to the room and the ability to wear the articles."

"Exactly. Miss Vanderbilt claimed she was retiring in her apartment at the time but did admit to having worn that dress that very night. If she had been an innocent woman who had happened upon the body, why would she lie and claim to be alone in her apartment? Why did she enter the alleyway and tear her ribbon?" I crossed my arms. "Either she is lying and therefore is the murderer or she is telling the truth and someone, which for our purposes tonight would have to be Mrs. Lewis, stole the dress and hat, did the deed. Once that was accomplished, she returned the clothes with the other planted evidence to the dressing room. Tell me, Captain," I said turning again to my friend, "was any further evidence of a wheelbarrow found behind Mr. Gonzales' house?"

"I'm afraid not. We did find some depressed grass behind the house which could have been caused by a wheelbarrow, but it was uncertain."

"As it was suggested earlier, the killer, one of the two women, could have used a wheelbarrow. She transported the dead man to the front of Mr. Gonzales' house. Once there, she dumped the body, hid the wheelbarrow behind the house, returned to the body, inserted the knife into the man's back, screamed, and ran away. As Mr. Gonzales and the neighbors gawked at the dead man, she quietly returned to the back alley and stole away the means by which she was able to carry the body."

The captain smiled, and simply said, "Go on."

"Did you ask both women about the wheelbarrow."

"Ah, yes," said the captain. "And as we did so, we were looking for any hint of surprise. Miss Vanderbilt reacted with absurdity. Why would she have a wheelbarrow? Where would she keep it? 'In my barn?' she had mockingly said. We checked with the theater owner and he confirmed the theater did not own a wheelbarrow.

"Mrs. Lewis, whose property was spread out over several acres, seemed confused why I would ask such a question, but immediately admitted to owning one. She did so without the slightest indication she was attempting to hide the fact. She suggested it must be in the barn, where we found it. Upon examination, the wheelbarrow's tire was consistent with both the tire tracks found in the front and back of Mr. Gonzales' house. We even found traces of clay in the tire tread matching the color of clay at the scene and on Mr. Lewis' right shoulder."

"And the typewriter? Did you ask the two women if they owned a typewriter?"

"Both denied either owning or having access to one."

It was relatively rare in those days to own a personal typewriter. I asked, "In the social spheres of either woman, who might be in possession of such a device? A lawyer, some nearby office?"

"Mrs. Lewis was a housewife who, according to her neighbors, and her own testimony, rarely left her home. Living where she did, far away from many other residences and certainly away from offices, I do think it unlikely she would have easy access to a typewriting machine."

"And Miss Vanderbilt?"

"Miss Vanderbilt, being in the city, had of course more opportunity to access such a device. Her gregarious disposition and tendency to rub shoulders with the rich and powerful also meant she had many acquaintances who would have potentially owned typewriters. When asked, however, she said she couldn't think of a single acquaintance who owned one."

"Mr. Edison, your watch workings are becoming a bit too organized. I'm wondering if there isn't a hidden set of gears below the more obvious ones," John said. "If Mr. Lewis was carried to the front of Mr. Gonzales' house, we can assume he was killed elsewhere. Was it the dressing room? Or was there evidence for any other location?"

Dr. Morgan said, "I believe the only logical place for the murder was Miss Vanderbilt's dressing room."

"How so?" someone asked. "The evidence seems planted to my mind."

The doctor turned to the captain. "The stain you

mentioned on the front of the man's vest and shirt, it was vomit, wasn't it?"

The captain nodded.

Dr. Morgan turned to his peers. "I just realized the importance of the vinegar smell which the captain said had greeted them upon entering the dressing room. Arsenic poisoning can induce vomiting. Vinegar water was used to remove the smell, I suspect." The doctor turned to the captain and asked, "Did the body have an unpleasant odor?"

"Yes," the captain said. "Due to an evening breeze and our distant proximity to the body, we didn't notice it that night, but the coroner did report a foul, gastric, and vinegarish smell."

"The place of death was the actress' dressing room. The smell of vomit proves it."

"But," said Otto, "in such a public place? Did she drag the body down the side aisle saying, 'Pardon the dead body?'" Otto laughed loudly. "Mind your legs, madam. Corpse on the move!" He laughed harder, shaking his fleshy cheeks. "Really."

"The sound from the performance no doubt concealed the sounds of the man as he choked on his own vomit. As for how she removed the body, you forget the room had an outer door that had once led to the outhouse. Surely, the murderer used that door to remove the body to the waiting wheelbarrow just outside. When she returned to leave the dress and hat, she bolted the door from the inside and left by the second door, the one leading through the theater. Either woman would have intimate knowledge of the theater and would have made sure to leave quietly and without being seen."

We had determined a few matters. Most particularly, the fact that the murder had occurred in the actress' dressing room. But also that the killer wanted to make it look as though the actress was the murderer. The question was, were the clues left by Mrs. Lewis to implicate Miss Vanderbilt, or were they left by Miss Vanderbilt herself to suggest someone else had an interest in framing her?

I stood. "Due to an independent witness attesting to the fleeing woman wearing that particular dress and bonnet, I do not think Mr. Gonzales is our concern here. Furthermore, we can safely say the woman in the red dress was the murderer because the small strip of red ribbon she left behind was found in the alleyway where the murderer alone would have travelled with the wheelbarrow. Since Mr. Gonzales is one of the three possible suspects, I submit we only have two left. It is clear whoever the murderer was, Miss Vanderbilt was intended to appear to be the murderer in the eyes of the police by several pieces of obvious evidence. And yet, we have the missing key and the wheelbarrow that seems to have been the device used to move Mr. Lewis' body. These two subtle pieces of evidence implicate Mrs. Lewis. So, gentlemen, who was the murderer? A spiteful wife who does away with her cheating husband and desires to frame his lover—albeit a little too boldly? Or perhaps it is the actress who wishes to rid herself of an inconvenient gadfly, whilst also implicating someone from her past whom she even now hates."

Captain Barnwell raised an eyebrow almost a full inch, and his mustache wiggled ever so slightly.

I turned to him and said, "You said Mrs. Lewis faintly recognized the actress, but could not place who or from where. You further stated the actress recognized the wife's name and immediately began to rail against her. However, you failed to inform us whether the actress recognized the wife's face."

"I failed at nothing, my dear Carl," the captain said with obvious amusement. "I simply wasn't asked that particular question. However, since your question is now implied, I shall answer it. When shown a photograph of Mrs. Lewis, she took one brief look and then, meeting our eyes, she said she was sure it was the woman always complaining and making trouble."

"Ah, but again," I said, "we have independent corroboration according to her neighbors that Mrs. Lewis rarely, if ever, left her house, which was a good distance from the theater— some six miles if I remember correctly. And yet, Miss Vanderbilt has come to loath her. Somehow, a woman who rarely leaves her house and lives some distance from the theater is said to regularly enter a place she has come to utterly despise." I cleared my throat and said, "Gentlemen, my attention has turned once more to the actress."

11

"But surely," Otto said before being silenced by the dismissive wave of my hand.

"All I ask is, for a moment, let us consider the possibility the murderer was the actress. Let us assume she loathed someone so much, she was willing to commit murder. But, the person she loathed was not Mr. Lewis; there were too many obvious clues for that. No, the actress may have been tired of Mr. Lewis, but she had no reason to kill him. There was no threat from him. Blackmail? She could blackmail him, but how would he blackmail her?

"I submit that the object of Miss Vanderbilt's loathing was none other than the dead man's wife. Why, Mrs. Lewis herself, said she had been an actress and a terrible drunk. The coincidence of professions is too much for my mind. Mrs. Lewis is some ten years older than Miss Vanderbilt which meant she was certainly an established actress when Miss Vanderbilt began her career. After all, her sister did say she was an actress of some renown. Mrs. Lewis was a person she no doubt looked up to.

"Perhaps they had a mentorship," I said, waving a single

finger. "A particularly one-sided mentorship. Mrs. Lewis, before her conversion, would have treated Miss Vanderbilt much as Miss Vanderbilt now treated those under her such as Mr. Gonzales—as mere workers fit only to do her every bidding. It follows the wife would have only the vaguest of memories of Miss Vanderbilt. Yet, as a disciple, Mrs. Lewis' cruel treatment would, no doubt, have created an indelible impression on the aspiring young actress. Remember, Mrs. Lewis admitted she was a cruel drunk. She probably mistreated a number of underlings without thought and now, without a solid memory.

"So, Miss Vanderbilt seduced Mr. Lewis, murdered him, and left the wheelbarrow to suggest with subtlety that Mrs. Lewis had overdone it by framing her with clues too obvious. Most ingenious, indeed!"

"You overreach!" said Otto in a boisterous voice.

"It is demonstrated beyond all possibility of contradiction," I countered.

"Indeed! And what clue led you to such a wild conclusion?"

"Four facts stand out and point me irrevocably in that direction," said I with absolute certainty.

The entire group had their eyes on me. I smiled.

"One, Mrs. Lewis had a devoted neighbor who would come to her after her husband left, thus providing for her an alibi for most nights, including the night of the murder. True, this neighbor didn't stay long enough to provide a solid alibi, but she did stay long enough—nine that evening, I believe—to seriously reduce the time needed for the multitude of preparations for the murder and the planted evidence.

"Two, as I just now mentioned, according to Mrs. Lewis and her sister, she had been a 'terrible drunk' during her acting days. It is quite possible she did something to hurt her younger colleague, but due to the drink, she only retained a vague recollection of her adoring protégé.

"Three, the murder could have only occurred in the dressing room. Dr. Morgan proved that point. The murderous act of ingesting poisoned tea required time and a certain willingness on the part of the victim. If it were the actress, Mr. Lewis surely would have entered the closed room and willingly partaken of the tea. If it had been his wife, he certainly would not have stayed for tea—not in the dressing room of his mistress, of this we can be sure. The wife could have killed him there by pistol, but certainly not the slow, agonizing poisoning of arsenic. The killer was Miss Vanderbilt. Of this, I have no doubt."

Otto crossed his arms in defiance. "I admit this is consistent and logical. However, there still lacks hard proof. Perhaps the wife doused him with some sleep inducing agent and then while he was asleep, poisoned him by force."

"Four," I said continuing despite my dear friend, Otto's, protestations. "Pay special attention to the ribbon that was found caught in the tree limb on the side of Mr. Gonzales' house and then consider the height of the women. Remember, we have already established the murderer had to have been the screaming woman in the red dress precisely because of the torn ribbon. The limb to which the piece of torn ribbon was attached stood a full six feet from the ground according to Captain Barnwell. The hat was said to be small, perhaps sitting no more than two inches from the top of the woman's head. This fact alone would have made it difficult for Mrs. Lewis to have hidden her long hair in—thick hair down to the small of her back as the captain had described it—but most importantly, the loose section of the ribbon, that flapped in the air as the woman fled, was said to be six inches from the hat. A five foot three inch woman, namely, Mrs. Lewis, wouldn't have been close enough for anything but the tip of the ribbon to be brushed by the limb. However, the five foot ten inch Miss Vanderbilt, was clearly tall enough to have snagged the ribbon."

I moved in front of the entire group. "Gentlemen, the killer could only have been Miss Vanderbilt."

Otto uncrossed his arms. Then, as if on his own road to Damascus, the scowl on his face converted to an unrestrained smile. Slapping his oversized belly, he let out a good laugh and said to Edison, "Too bad, old chap. Carl has gone and smashed your watch!"

"*Au contraire*," I said. "Edison's analogy was perfectly accurate. The positioning of clues in such precise order was evidence of a mind behind it. However, the clues which implicated Miss Vanderbilt were obvious and loud. The clues, the missing key and the found wheelbarrow, the ones the actress hoped would lead to Mrs. Lewis, were far subtler. The still small voice, gentlemen. We were meant to come to a singular conclusion, but not go a step further."

Edison said, "Well, then, Captain, did you confront Miss Vanderbilt with these points? And was she the murderer?"

The captain spent a few moments in a stoic silence. Then, quite suddenly, the tips of his mustache turned upward, the hairs forming a rising theater curtain, unveiling and indicating the end of the final act, *the Captain's Play*. The smile turned into a roaring laughter, a kind of hearty laughter I had never heard before nor after from my friend.

"Yes, you are quite correct," he said after a few moments to compose himself. "She did indeed murder Mr. Lewis with the intent to implicate the wife. But I must say, Carl, that was very clever of you to work out the connection between the two women's past."

"It was your facial hair," I said with a slight twinkling in my eye.

"My facial hair? How so?"

"Your mustache moved. The movement was slight, yes, but significant. Furthermore, upon hearing my theory that the actress acted on her desire to implicate someone from her past, you arched your eyebrow. Your facial hair showed my hypothesis to be true."

The captain laughed even harder than before.

"You'd make a good police officer, Mr. Brooke. It is indeed quite important to hear not only the facts, but to ferret out cues and clues from the presenter as well. Yes, your guess was correct. I was waiting for one of you to ask me of that connection.

"As it transpires, Mrs. Lewis' stage name had been Lizzie Eames when Miss Vanderbilt knew her. She had indeed been something of a popular attraction at the Adelphi. After Mrs. Lewis' dramatic departure, the theater was in great need of a new headliner. At the behest of the Adelphi managers, young Vanderbilt took her mentor's name and material. Unfortunately, Mrs. Lewis' fans did not appreciate her efforts, and the later Miss Vanderbilt was unceremoniously booed off the stage and counted as a fraud by the papers.

"Despite having had her managers' permission—indeed it had been their idea—she was let go and spent several penniless months between jobs until finding work at the St. James Theatre. After several stage name changes, she finally found the kind of success she had always desired. But, she never forgot her earlier embarrassment. She blamed that squarely on Mrs. Lewis.

"Mr. Lewis was nothing more than a hapless pawn chosen by Miss Vanderbilt to affect revenge on her old mentor and then nemesis."

The captain spread wide his arms and said, "Gentlemen, congratulations on a fine piece of detective work."

According to Captain Barnwell, Mrs. Lewis took the betrayal and murder of her husband terribly hard, following him to the grave in a matter of months. Mr. Gonzales, on the other hand, enjoyed a wide readership of his serialized account of the matter in the Boston Tribune. While I have my suspicions regarding their real names, I never asked the captain to confirm them.

Captain Barnwell came before us that evening expecting us to not accept the first conclusion that came to our minds, namely that Miss Vanderbilt had been the guilty party. But, the truth wasn't even found in the second step. Several steps removed, we finally returned again to the murderer.

The lesson is clear. One should always think beyond the present, beyond the obvious. Hard truth can only come by hard and deliberate effort. As the Good Book says: "The simple believeth every word: but the prudent man looketh well to his going."

It is a truism for all the ages.

AFTERWORD

I really hope you enjoyed The Agora Letters. If you did, please look for other Agora mysteries (search: "Agora Clay Boutwell").

This book would not have been possible if not for the kind help of my Beta readers. This august group (not unlike the *Agora Society* members) selflessly gave up time to help make this a better book than it would have been otherwise. They often found the most embarrassing mistakes and reported these mistakes to me with a kindness that barely left a dent on my shockingly thin skin. (I'm working on that.)

A few names I wish to thank in particular, but in no particular order, are:

- Rebecca Andreasen
- Kerry Donovan
- The Woloszyn Clan (especially Ellie, Cookie, and Lydia)
- Yoni & Dany Abreu
- Mark & Apple McDow

- David and Janelis Overholt
- Anna & Daniel Strand
- Derice Harwood
- Wanda Aasen
- Dawn Keene
- And last but not least, my sister, Pam Touchton.

--

Please contact the author at clay@clayboutwell.com or visit his blog at: http://www.ClayBoutwell.com

Your comments and questions are most welcome.

ALSO BY CLAY BOUTWELL

THE AGORA MYSTERY SERIES

All mysteries are stand-alone stories.

The Agora Letters - For the first time, get the first five stories in the Agora Series in a single volume at a reduced price.

Two Tocks before Midnight - When a flurry of forgeries appear in museums and among collectors, the members of the Agora, a society dedicated to the betterment of man, take it upon themselves to stop the rogues.

The Penitent Thief - A string of thefts ends in a grisly murder. Certain evidence leads Captain Barnwell to suspect a former thief, Rutherford Nordlinger as the culprit. Carl Brooke becomes personally involved as Nordlinger's guilt is questioned.

The Peace Party Massacre - Kidnapped! An honorable man has gone missing and his wife is not in the least helpful. The sheriff dithers and every day brings death closer to a reality.

The Curse of the Mad Sheik - A grieving widow believes her husband's death to be something more than a failing heart. A ruby— said to be cursed—had been found in his hands. The police and her closest kin say otherwise.

The Captain's Play - Captain Barnwell, long an honorary member of the Agora Society, presents to the members a solved case one clue at a time. Three suspects. One is the murderer.

Murder by Monday - A mysterious letter sends Carl Brooke and Rutherford Nordlinger off to the aid of a man who, accused of murder, is now threatened by the man he is said to have killed.

Eggs Over Arsenic - An art critic is brutally murdered and the subject of his last review is suspected. Did the artist do it or was it one of the family members--all of whom had motive and opportunity?

THE TEMPORAL SERIES

The Temporal — A devastating earthquake in central Japan sends eternity crashing into time, enabling Sam to hear echoes of the past and even the future. Through the echoes, Sam and a mysterious Japanese woman learn of a terrorist plot that could plunge the world into turmoil and position a murderer as the leader of the free world.

A Temporal Trust — After stopping a terrorist plot to position a murderer as president, Sam Williams must come to grips with his newfound abilities. As one of the Temporal, his encounters with eternity give him both gifts and challenges to overcome as a new threat emerges that could wipe out the Temporal for all time.

Carritos — In 1906, the San Francisco earthquake took everything from Jackson. It took, but it also gave. He soon found he had been given the ability **to...stop time,** to "freeze" the world around him. He lives the good life among tiny mortals. Stealing, bribing, stumbling his way into making a living. All this can be forgiven, he figures, as long as he keeps two rules. Just two, but they are absolute and non-negotiable: *thou shalt not kill and family comes first.* Now

Jackson must make a choice, a choice that will change everything. **The choice is: which rule will he break?**

THE TANAKA SERIES

Tanaka and the Yakuza's Daughter — Akira Tanaka's past as an undercover agent in Tokyo's underworld has caught up with his present. Now he must find out who kidnapped his only daughter, and why. Can he rescue her before it's too late?

Made in the USA
Middletown, DE
14 August 2018